Australia
y works
cluding
Hodder
ring her
of the
Home.
oetry is
'ing" in

AVERY®   L7160™

This book must be
returned to
Colaiste Iognaid
Sea Road, Galway

Praise for *Rift*

'*Complex but not complicated . . . Rift draws you in with its seductive plot and carefully structured characters.*' Viewpoint

'*Beats your average adult novel for sensuous detail, drama and a good, gripping narrative.*' Melbourne Age

'*A good, racy story . . . The fantasy is terrifyingly possible, the narrative never loses momentum and the complexity of the human relationships is never glossed over.*' Courier-Mail

'*A real page-turner.*' Geelong Advertiser

'*Ms Hathorn's best book yet . . . I read it in one long sitting and it gripped me from the first page . . . powerful.*' Bookchat

Rift

Libby Hathorn

Hodder
Children's
Books

a division of Hodder Headline plc

For Rod the Brave

Copyright © 1998 Enterprises Pty Limited

First published by arrangement with Hodder Headline
Australia Pty Limited Australia and New Zealand in 1998
by Hodder Headline Australia
First published in Great Britain in 1999
by Hodder Children's Books

10 9 8 7 6 5 4 3 2 1

Visit Libby Hathorn's website at: http://www.libbyhathorn.com

A CIP catalogue record for this book is available from
the British Library

ISBN 0 340 74410 3

Offset by Avon Dataset Ltd, Bidford-on-Avon, Warks

Printed and bound in Great Britain by
The Guernsey Press Co. Ltd, Channel Islands

Hodder Children's Books
a division of Hodder Headline plc
338 Euston Road
London NW1 3BH

ONE

He'd watched the Settlement boys for weeks now. They clambered over the volcanic rock bare-footed, never flinching. Hard little splinters and needles of stone bruised and battered his own pale feet. Drew blood. The boys of the Settlement ran sure-footed.

Vaughan had tried to speak to them on the first day but they ran by, a hard knot of boys together. He was an outsider and he soon knew outsider he'd remain these summer holidays unless…unless what?

Unless he did the dive. And that, well, that seemed pretty near impossible.

■

'Vaughan Jasper Roberts the Third. That's you! That's my boy!'

Another contender for the Roberts' name, the Roberts' fame, his father had joked. Seeking fame even now, his father was strumming his guitar outside their seedy motel room, preparing for the equally seedy club gig that would provide him with not much more than drinking money.

The afternoon was flecked with gold, handfuls of leaves cascading down from English-looking trees that had given the motel its name—The Oaks.

'Shitloads of 'em,' as his father had so gracefully put it, mellowed out, an early morning mood. Vaughan had thrown handfuls of autumn at Vivien, his mum, and she'd loved it, standing still a moment, girlish in her burnished yellow fuzzy jumper and navy jogging pants, her palms turned up like a kid, as if expecting a prize, a kiss, a gift.

Then she'd shovelled handfuls of leaves, made them cascade through the air all over them, as if there were some bright golden road that linked the three of them. Rare and precious moments of Vaughan's happiness.

His father not drunk yet and his mother happy. He thought the burnished gold leaves just about the same colour as her hair.

Vaughan had come to hate that line by the end of the trip, the one about the Roberts' name, the Roberts' fame. His father exhausted, angry, his mother removed from Jasper, his dad, but removed from him too. From her only son. He'd got measles and they'd had to forgo the town where she was sure she was going to get her big break. The very town.

'A big kid like you getting a bloody baby disease—and right now!' It was his father who had looked after him, brought him cool drinks and bathed his forehead in those spotty days in the cheapest of cheap motels where he sweated it out until fit enough to go on again.

■

The saying 'swim like a fish' was so right for these kids. They *were* fish! Sleek, seaworthy, salt-sea hardy. Diving and rolling and playing. Dive-bombing each other or riding waves like real sea creatures. Browned by the sun. He burnt so badly the first afternoon down at the rocks his grandmother made him wear a T-shirt after that, just as if he was a little kid!

'And don't go wandering off without telling me—there's work to do you know!'

But the sound of the boys' harsh cries as they passed by the lonely house drew him out a short while later, drew him out every afternoon despite her warnings. 'There are some ruffians who hang about the Devil's Head. Don't you go and get involved or you'll be gone all summer with those tearaways.'

He'd like to be a ruffian and a tearaway but was more likely a wimp compared to them and he knew it. Rubber thongs to protect his feet from the rocks. A T-shirt to protect his shoulders from the sun. His grandmother had even given him a pair of sunglasses. But none of the Settlement kids wore sunglasses and he'd planned to hide them somewhere in a rock crevice as he climbed out along the rock platform to watch.

On the fourth day he'd followed them, one of the boys stopped on the beach and took a pee by a huge pillar, one of the upthrusts of rock that happened unexpectedly round here. Vaughan, rounding a sandhill, saw him down on the flat and the boy waved to him. It was just a curt acknowledgment. Not a smile. Just a wave, but Vaughan felt his heart lift. The first real feeling of pleasure he'd known since coming to live in this God-forsaken seaside town with his complaining grandmother. The gesture gave him the courage to go closer to the knot of boys skylarking on the rocks and in the water of the bay. Their place, not his. Okay, he knew that well enough already. But maybe he could belong.

Vaughan stayed back in the shadow of a cluster of those looming rocks, watching. There seemed to be a ritual. The boys would play in the water for an hour, sometimes more. Then they'd all get out. Vaughan never saw a signal, heard a sound, but with one accord the boys would line up on the spiked volcanic rock surface. Vaughan was jealously aware of the stature of each of them. The one who'd waved to him, and another boy, one who seemed to be the leader, looked a few years older than the others. They both had powerful chests and arm muscles that bespoke their manhood. But even those other younger boys—slender and wiry—looked strong. Vaughan knew that in a few years, maybe only a year, they'd more than likely end up looking like their athletic leader.

Vaughan would climb out along the rocky ledge, leap across a few pools and then take the high climb to the jutting, overbearing rock that seemed to bow to another opposite it. Here he could watch the boys without fear of being seen. They would sit silent and still for some moments. Then one of them, a different boy each time, would stand. The first day, when the first boy lowered his head between his arms, his body a smooth spear of intent, Vaughan realised he was about to make a dive. He almost cried out, for surely he would dive headfirst onto rock.

But no, that was ridiculous! There was the sound of the body hitting water and then nothing. Now the line of boys stood and they walked the full length of the jutting rock slowly and silently. Not a word, no noisy jostling as there had been minutes earlier. They stood in a semi-circle at the opposite end and waited. There was a terrible tension in the air. Vaughan waited too.

Surely the diver would have surfaced by now? No one could hold his breath so long. He must be beside the rock out there in the less than playful surf, battling his way to the other end. But as Vaughan climbed higher to look down on what they were watching he saw the small, jewel blue pond. Its still surface suddenly broke as the head of a boy, the diver, burst out of the water, his face a gargoyle of effort and then smiles as he sent waves lapping to the black rock. Screams and hoots and victory yells and laughter came from up top. The boys jostled each other to be the one to reach down for the swimmer and pull him up out of the water onto the rocks.

It occurred to Vaughan that the diver must have swum an incredible 80 metres under the rock, surely not under the water? A secret passage through the rock? But what were they doing now? A strange Settlement ritual was taking place and the diver was being honoured in some way. The others formed a semi-circle and the big boy, the leader, placed a wreath or something that looked like a wreath, on the diver's head. There was a silence for a few moments. They didn't exactly bow down to the diver but

their heads were lowered. The diver took off the wreath—
hard to see what it was, but a circle of green—and held it
aloft for thrilling moments. And then he chucked it as hard
as he could. Vaughan watched the circlet fly high into the
air before it went down, down. Not back into the pool from
where the boy had emerged but into the part of the cliff
where he'd first started. Back where the surging surf
clawed at the silver-black, ever wet rock.

Late that afternoon Vaughan went down to inspect the
place where the boy had made the dive. Through deep
water and way over the other side, when the water was
sucked back, he saw the mouth of what must be a lone
cave. It was hung with ribbons of seaweed and he realised
then what the wreath had been made of.

Vaughan stripped and dived into the small pool, inspect-
ing the entrance of the cave where the water heaved and
lolloped. He tried to swim inside even a few metres but the
water was rough and beyond the slimy seaweed was a terrible dark. He was glad to pull himself up out of the pool
that felt more like a hole now, and away from the gaping
cave mouth. That's what it felt like to him, a mouth that
would snap shut should he enter it. And yet the boys did!

Not every afternoon, but at least once a week, one of the
small group performed the same amazing stunt. The quiet-
ness surrounding the dive, the exhilaration of the greeting
when the chosen one had surfaced once again and the
same ritual of the wreath followed. Vaughan took to counting the seconds, his heart thudding as if indeed he were
the one swimming for dear life through the rock tunnel. It
was too long to hold your breath. Far too long. Perhaps
there was an air pocket down there? Must be. He watched

hungrily as the others paid homage to the diver from the moment he emerged, silently congratulating him too. And when they'd gone, noisy and hooting and playful, he had his daydream. Saw himself as the diver, the chosen one, making the difficult and the exulting lone dive. And being one of the group, victorious at the end of it.

■

'If you want to join Liam and the others you gotta do the Tunnel—Devil's Gullet we call it. Gotta swim through the Devil's Arsehole—our joke!' The boy who'd waved at him that afternoon, Rodney Chi, was friendly when he was on his own. Vaughan met him one afternoon surfing at Mad-shark. Rod was quick to explain Liam's rules.

'Liam's the big one?' Vaughan asked Rod.

'Yeah, the *other* big one.' And Rod laughed again. 'Too big now to get through the tunnel easy. Too big for the middle bit.'

'So can I join you, the others?'

'Yeah, but only the dive'll get you in.'

They sat surveying the restless body of water, the sharp flips of spray that flew up every now and then with no recognisable rhythm to them. 'And it's not all that bloody easy either,' Rod warned, 'But not impossible—if you like underwater swimming, that is.'

'I'm not that good a swimmer,' Vaughan stammered.

'You want in?'

Yes he wanted in. He nodded.

'Then you'd better learn to be a good swimmer. Can you dive okay?'

'Yeah, I can dive but only in the Council swimming baths at home. And they weren't all that close, so I'm not that good,' Vaughan was at pains to explain, both glad and worried that he'd been invited so easily.

'If you want in,' Rod shrugged, 'I could help. Bit of training, that's all you need. My cousin's got gear. Underwater stuff. That'll help for starters. And I'm an instructor. We could go through the lessons if you want. Then you can take a look round, know what it's all about down there with the gear. But you gotta do the tunnel without any gear. Up to you, though.'

'I dunno.'

Days, all the days, of Vaughan's holidays and beyond stretched before him. Down at the Settlement alone. The months and years stretched ahead of him. Why was that, when his parents had promised they were coming back in a few weeks? But the sense of time yawning up ahead had a vice-like grip. At school, when school started in a few weeks, he'd be alone. At home he'd be alone, his grandmother immobile in front of the flickering screen, glass of amber in hand, complaining tongue at the ready. He couldn't bear the thought of it, of not belonging.

He told Rod he'd think about it and walked back up the sandhill, kicking the soft sand as he went. In the main street there was always sand underfoot too. The town was airless. Awnings and tired shop entrances parched white, so many of the shops half-heartedly boarded up to indicate their closure. Must have closed years ago now. Vaughan had felt an oppression the moment he'd set eyes on the town. And it wasn't only to do with the fact that his parents were so far away and he not easy with his grandmother who'd grudgingly taken him in.

The place reeked of something. Not the fish that had been the livelihood of the town—an industry that was slowly dying. It reeked of something else. Despair? Humiliation? Failure maybe? He didn't like the look of the place anyway. Didn't want to frame the word that had actually sprung to mind immediately. Fear. But even that wasn't quite right. Restlessness maybe. Well, the constant wind was restless that was for sure. Darkness. Something. Something hopeless.

Then there was the creaking weatherboard house where his grandmother lived. 'Nicely situated close to Madshark Cove,' his father had placated him. 'You'll have your grandmother for company. Golden opportunity to get to know her. Funny old duck but not too bad you know, once you get to understand her. And there's Madshark and that's the greatest place.'

His father was right about Madshark, with its wonder of an isthmus of sand that came and went, a surf to either side of you if you walked its centre. Vaughan had heard about it for years, just as he'd heard about how his grandmother would make a fuss of him. She had, but not in the way Vaughan wanted. His grandmother seemed to want to know his every move. He wasn't used to that at all with his own parents. They were rarely interested and it seemed he was the one usually trailing them. But his grandmother insisted on keeping tabs of his comings and goings.

Just as she'd insisted he go to the church to meet the new Pastor she seemed to be growing so attached to. He'd gone only to appease her on his first weekend there. It was

not like any church he'd ever known. He hadn't understood the strange chanting and the joining of hands which
seemed to bring such an intensity to all the others in the
congregation. And he hadn't liked meeting the pale, flickering blue eyes of the sandy-coloured Pastor. Yeah, that
man seemed to suit the place all right. Sand-coloured hair,
reddish grey eyebrows, his characterless clay-coloured
safari suit a grim concession to the flagrant summer here.
Vaughan hadn't liked the man's voice either, with its booming American overtones. Or those dirges followed by
incomprehensible tides of enthusiasm that only seemed to
make Vaughan feel that he was fading into invisibility,
receding like the tide out there.

Later, thinking about the overlong service, he couldn't
figure out why he tasted metal the minute that voice began,
and on its rising inflections saw scattered images of war, the
Pastor's face mad with desire for it. Perhaps it was because
his grandmother had explained so proudly that the Pastor
had fought in the Vietnam War. He didn't care. The church
and the Pastor were not for him and he let her know it
quick smart.

TWO

'That new kid, Vaughan what's-his-name. He's okay, mate.'

Rod and Liam climbed out of the deep sea pool where they'd been practising their spear fishing.

'He looks like a little kid,' Liam said.

'He's fifteen!'

'Squirt.' Liam lay back on the warm rock, his tanned skin gleaming in the morning sun. He shook his blond hair. 'So he could fit through the Devil's Gullet okay? Bet he doesn't have the guts!'

They sat on the rock together, looking beyond the pool to where the surf fought its way up the rocks, ready any minute to spill over.

'He's not all that strong a swimmer, and he reckons he's only here for the summer. Why don't you let him into the gang? He's kind of lost, and he's okay.'

But Rod saw the line of Liam's determined jaw. 'No

losers, you know that. Every kid has had a go at it—even Sandy. And all of them, even the little squirts, made it in the end.'

'Yeah, but Sandy panicked and backed off and you still let him in.'

'It's the rule,' Liam insisted. 'That new kid, tell him he should have a go at the Gullet—and then we'll see.' Liam stood up and gathered his gear.

'Where you off to?' Rod was surprised. They usually spent a whole afternoon together, fooling around in the surf and on the beach after their dives.

'Don't laugh but I'm going up to the church.'

'You're what!'

'Patrick and a couple of the fellas from our street are helping me do a paint job up there.'

'How much an hour?'

Liam stared down at Rod, 'There's no money involved.'

'What—kindness of your heart sort of thing?' and Rod laughed.

'You could say.'

'Wonders never cease!'

'Look, Patrick's changed a lot and he reckons the Pastor man's okay. I know we thought it was a whole load of rubbish that night we went there. But the Pastor's not too bad when you get to talk to him one to one. Not bad at all.'

'Patrick's a loser if ever there was one.' Rod was confused. Patrick wasn't the kind of person Liam would normally spend time with.

'I said I'd help out there and I will.'

'Mind if I don't come with you,' Rod couldn't help the note of annoyance in his voice.

'Have a nice day,' Liam quipped, smiling down a friend, unperturbed.

Rod watched Liam making his way up the rock face and disappear over the sandhill. He felt disappointed, deflated. It seemed that things had changed between them over the last few weeks and even over the last few days. Liam was always off somewhere, not keen to spend time with him the way he usually did.

Liam and the church! Jesus Mary and Joseph he'd had enough of churches when his father had been alive. Was Liam going all religious or what? It was incredible to think of him up there in perfect diving weather, painting the ramshackle old building to please a fly-by-night Pastor.

'An imposter of a man if ever I've seen one,' Rod's mother, Rhonda Chi, had commented, making herself unpopular with some of the Pastor's followers at the small high school where she was the English and history teacher.

With his promises for a brighter future, the Pastor had gained a modest but quite devoted band of followers as soon as he arrived. They'd worked with him tirelessly at the old church and then in the Compound where he'd taken up residence.

The Compound, so called because of a wire fence that had once separated it from the rest of the town, had been a workers' camp site. Someone had had the foresight or the cunning, perhaps encouraged by the town's publican, to build the long low huts and the odd bungalow with a hotel right at the centre. Here the beer and the comradeship flowed freely for the men who lived in the barracks, forging new roads to the site of the dam they were building. And then, as quickly as the Compound had been established, it had closed down, the dam completed. Wind and sand and neglect had meant the buildings and roads had soon fallen into disrepair. But the Pastor had leased the land and was already talking of making the Compound come to life once again, with the large rambling Powers' Pub becoming a Centre for Philosophy and Religious teaching.

The Pastor talked of a great company of people throughout America who were supporting him and indeed supporting any of them who wished to be part of it, this brave, new venture. The Compound seemed a strange venue indeed, in a town where the population was clearly decreasing. But the Pastor obviously had backing, and spent money freely to reclaim the place. He didn't seem to mind the lonely situation by the beach. In fact, more than once he commented on the beauty of isolation from the pace and distractions of the outside world, wonderful for a community such as theirs.

And now Liam was taking an interest in it all. He was a funny one, Rod reflected, gazing moodily out to the breakers. He'd known him three years now. Three years since the Chi family—Rod, his half-sister Nona and their mother, Rhonda—had come to the Settlement, where Rhonda had a job. He'd been brought here 'kicking and screaming', as his mother had put it. But in those three years a friendship had blossomed between him and Liam, a friendship that had in some way compensated for Rod not being able to be part of the dive school he wanted to join in a much larger seaside town.

In one way you could get only so close to Liam, Rod thought. And lately, in these last few weeks since Nona had been secretly going out with Liam, Rod felt even more on the outer. Whole afternoons had been given over to Nona. Afternoons that took his friend away from Madshark and all their usual haunts.

It was strange, Rod reflected, that Liam would not let Nona anywhere near the Gullet during the ritual dive that had become, over the months and years, more or less central to his life. More than once, curious, Nona had asked Rod about what actually took place there.

'Liam was in the cadets at school and he kind of models the training he does with the young boys on army stuff. Only more so.'

'But you hate all that, don't you?' Nona couldn't hide her surprise that Rod would take part in any such thing.

'I put up with it because I like diving with him. And if that's the way he wants to do it...I don't really give a shit. The boys seem to like it. They think he's making them tough! And I suppose he is. Daring anyway.'

'He's reckless all right!' and Nona's eyes shone in a way that worried her half-brother. 'It's so important to him to keep this thing going too,' she mused.

'What thing?' But he knew before she answered.

'The ritual dive—for you-know-who,' she'd answered. Rod had been sworn to secrecy and had never discussed Liam's 'trouble' with anyone, least of all his sister who might well divulge things to their mother. Now he realised she and Liam must already be very close.

Rod was annoyed. He'd thought only *he* knew the unutterable importance of the dive in Liam's life, just as he knew Liam was obsessive about it. In fact, Liam was obsessive about many of the things he did. Maybe that was why

Rod was attracted to him as a friend. He seemed a person of such extremes. And the good times with Liam were so good. Never mind his strange and unaccountable fits of temper from time to time. Well, now he was telling Nona secret things too, and Rod didn't like it.

'He's taking me out with the Nooan boys. He's training some of them to dive and he said he'd instruct me in that dive course,' Nona had announced.

'I'm a fully qualified instructor, you know that!' Rod was extremely proud of the intensive Padi diving course he'd taken, and miffed that she was suddenly so interested. 'I'll teach you if you want. You said you didn't like underwater stuff.'

Nona smiled at him, looking older than her barely sixteen years. 'It's okay, Rod,' she was being almost sympathetic, as if she guessed something of his aggrievement. 'Liam's got this beginners' thing going. He's a good teacher. Thorough—we have to do tests, you know. But it's fun too!'

'You better not let Mum know you're hanging out with them!' He hadn't added his annoyance at being left out of the equation altogether.

'She'll have to learn to live with it,' Nona had answered and there was almost something Liam-like in the way she said it.

The Nooan boys were taking up Liam's time this summer too, Rod reflected, slowly packing up his own gear and wondering about the long stretch of afternoon before him. He'd lost his part-time job at Clemen's Garage and he wasn't only missing the money. Liam was thick with the Nooan boys now, spending more and more time with them.

Rod's mother hadn't liked the way Liam had introduced her son to the so-called Nooan boys. They were 'home' boys from another town up north. There was no shame in that, she'd said, but a number of them had recently come into the Settlement and taken a house just out of the town by the beach. Most of the townspeople were suspicious of what transpired there.

The Nooan Homes had been closed down after an unfavourable government report, the younger boys dispersed to other refuges and the older ones told to move on, there being nothing in the town for them. They were advised to break up the group to better their chances of employment. But they'd stuck together, come as a group to the Settlement, half-heartedly talking about getting a fishing boat. This hadn't eventuated but they'd settled in by the beach, and very soon the inhabitants of the town had cause for complaint. The noise of their music, their drug habits, the motorbikes they'd purchased, trouble with the police. The obvious disapproval hadn't worried the Nooan boys—in fact they seemed to thrive on it, swaggering through the town together, aware of the admiring glances from some of the younger boys of the town, the fearful looks from others.

'Why come here to this dead hole?' Rod had quizzed Liam after the first meeting with the group. He sensed a tension in Liam he didn't quite understand. As if the Nooan boys were Liam's 'property'. 'Cat Harbour's bigger and surely it's better further up the coast! That's where I'm heading soon as I can.'

'Cheap as chips here, the house and everything,' Liam

explained. 'And the surf's the best! Cat Harbour hasn't got a surf near as good. They reckon it's real cool here.'

It was well known the boys shared their housekeeping, such as it was, pooling their dole cheques. 'Hell, they're bringing their dollars into the town so why anybody's complaining...'

'I'm not narrow-minded like a lot of them round here,' Rhonda had told her son, 'but they do a lot of sitting around and smoking and they make no attempt to work—any of them. They're all able-bodied young men. They could attempt to learn something. Even to help with the fishing, if they intend staying round here. Look, I don't care about them drawing the dole, like some of the others round here do, but they're so indolent. And that's going to lead them into trouble.'

'Maybe they need time,' Rod had defended them. 'They've had a hell of a life in the Home, according to Liam. And anyway, they're learning scuba diving! Every one of them. That's something.' His mother always insisted on the importance of learning.

'With what in mind?' she'd retorted.

'Scuba diving, Mum! Bloody scuba diving! What else!' He'd left the house wondering why he felt so explosive about what she said to him these days. Wondering whether it might not be better to be part of the Nooan's household and not to have to answer to anyone. But no. The boys answered to each other for sure. And now, he was certain, to Liam as well.

Sitting in the sun by himself, gazing into the depths of the empty pool, Rod had to admit he felt jealous of the Nooan boys and the way Liam had taken them under his wing. Or in truth, he was jealous of the way they followed Liam, hanging on to his every word. That's why Rod felt an immediate sympathy for the new boy in town, young Vaughan Roberts, who was trailing after the gang. In a way, Rod was trailing after Liam this summer, whereas once it had been the two of them, *leading* the others.

Rod gathered up his gear. Maybe he'd go home. But there was doom and gloom there right now, his mother learning her school was likely to be closing due to falling numbers. She'd been waiting for news of her contract for weeks and was already poring over the newspapers for new positions, tense and anxious. No, he wouldn't go there just yet, he'd go over to Madshark by himself. Sometimes some of the boys were there.

There was a lone surfer. Someone he couldn't recognise at first and then, as the boy came out of the surf waving at him, he realised it was Vaughan. Vaughan *Roberts*, of course, same name as the boy's grandmother, old Mrs Roberts.

'What you got there?' Vaughan was shy, but not too shy. He came straight up to Rod and sat beside him on the sand.

'Been spear fishing,' Rod told him. 'Liam and me—'

'D'you think he'll let me in with you lot? Did he say?'

'He reckons you should try the Devil's Gullet, same as everybody.'

'How long would it take to learn to make a dive like that one?'

'Couple of weeks—I said I'd show you. Anyway, I can take you through a diving course you know.' Rod was thinking of Liam and Nona. 'I'm a qualified instructor.'

'That'd be cool. But the dive, under those rocks…holding your breath that long…'

'Once you get the hang of scuba diving you'll get confidence, you'll find the dive easier. Deadset!'

Vaughan hesitated, but Rod ploughed on. 'Meet you here tomorrow arvo. Start the training straight off. Breath control and all of that. It'll come to you real fast, I swear it! Don't think about it too much. It'll be easy, you'll see.'

'I don't know…'

'Sure you do. See you tomorrow.'

Rod felt a little more light-hearted as he headed for home. But Vaughan, heading for more of his grandmother's rousing, felt uneasy, as if the die had been cast and there was no going back.

THREE

The house, the sea, the wind at night, it was a place that made you dream. Vaughan's grandmother was restless, making tea in the early hours. He'd been roused by the quiet chink of crockery, thought of his parents for long moments, and then drifted back to sleep.

There was an underwater tunnel before him and as he moved through it the light faded bit by bit until he was swimming in a terrible suffocating blackness. Something lurked in the shadows, monstrous, gawping, waiting for him, he knew it. But the tunnel was way too small for him to turn back. He had to struggle onward against an impossible current, on the watch for a monster he could not quite discern. When he felt the first of its limp tentacles reach for his face, the slimy connection was an electric shock. He awoke, sure he'd yelled out, to find the tangled sheet and the doona twisted over his head. This was the second time he'd dreamed of that tunnel and he realised he'd be haunted by it unless he took on the dive as soon as he could.

The dawn broke with the sound of seabirds and the gentle plash of waves. Must be low tide he thought, pleased that he was 'reading the water' the way his father said he had as a kid growing up here. Vaughan didn't like the Settlement, not the way his father had promised he would. But being in this derelict old house with January, his grandmother, terse as she was with him, there was some sort of comfort while his parents were so far away. Except for the dreamlife here. Maybe it was the wind and all that sand constantly distressed and churning.

No more dark dreams then, he thought, as he heard the comforting clatter of cutlery and china out in the old kitchen. He rose to complaining tones, 'I've had your breakfast ready, Vaughan, for half an hour!'

■

'How will you train me, then?' he asked Rod when they met next afternoon, trekking across the white sandhills to a secret destination.

'What?' Rod was scanning the beach.

'How will you teach me so's I can do the dive?' Vaughan repeated, his shock of dark hair flopping over anxious eyes as they strode across the beach.

'First, the fun bit,' Rod shot a smile at the younger boy. 'Taking you right round the bay, out to Lonely Place. Just checking no one's watching us go, that's all.'

'Why?' Vaughan asked, though he already knew Liam disapproved of him and would until he'd had a go at the dive.

'Don't want anyone snooping,' Rod answered easily. Then he added, 'And I told Liam we'd be the only ones to use the place. The gear too! Kind of exclusive, if you know what I mean.'

Vaughan wondered why Rod needed Liam's approval but didn't ask.

'My cousin James and I called it Lonely Place,' he told Vaughan. 'It's a kind of code for when we went scuba diving, and we didn't want anyone else to know what we were up to. Lonely Place meant we'd meet here in the shed. Use the gear for a dive.'

'Are we diving today?' Vaughan couldn't keep the excitement out of his voice.

'Beginners' course.' Rod was unzipping canvas bags and taking out wetsuits and scuba diving gear. Vaughan didn't know what to say but Rod was already handing him the equipment.

'See, my cousin James put me through a training course. A world famous one, called Padi. I've got my certificate now.'

'Yeah?'

'He left all his gear when he went. So I can train you same way.'

'For the dive?'

'Yes and no. Just to get a feel for underwater first of all. Breathing underwater with the gear. And seeing the world that's down there, a world you could never imagine. Not in a million years. It's—well—wait until you see it.'

The big boy was obviously keen to share this secret

world with the new kid on the block and Vaughan was silently grateful. But he was frightened, too. What if he didn't measure up? And what about the underwater stint at that other place he'd still have to do?

But there was no question of fear with Rod teaching him. The minute Vaughan pulled on the mask and put his face under the surface he felt a fish-like affinity with that underwater place.

Over the summer days Rod took him through the safety procedures with painstaking rigour: the buddy system if air failed; the sign system for up and down and for help; the art of inflating the wetsuit so that you rose easily to the surface; what to do if you came face to face with a shark. 'Called the place Madshark for a reason I reckon!' Rod had joked one afternoon as he went though the drill again with supreme patience.

He took Vaughan through all the gear, all the rules that would make the dive not only more successful but 'safe as'.

'We're talking life and death you know, down there, so you gotta know your stuff.'

Through the long summer afternoons of training, Vaughan thought he hadn't been as happy in a long time— until they actually ventured out to *see* some of the underwater wonders.

Rod had described the dives they would do over a few weeks, going further as Vaughan became more skilled. They would explore a deep sea channel outside the reef where massive schools of fish congregated, and then the Coral Wall with its pelagics and massive clams, the iridescent reef fish that would be the highlight. Even the shorter dives close to the safety of the jetty where it was much more shallow, sounded spectacular. Yet as Rod had hinted, nothing could really prepare Vaughan for the impact of his first proper dive and the marvel of that underwater world.

It took place on a brilliant afternoon, the horizon empty. No boats, no whales in sight, just a sea to themselves. Vaughan followed Rod down and down. After the realisation that he was breathing, actually breathing easily deep underwater, it seemed to Vaughan the closest thing to flying that anyone could do. Skimming over the convolutions of coral, the brain and soft corals, reef fish, barrel sponges, Vaughan felt he'd been allowed entry into another world. A magic world! They moved surely, like sea things themselves, until Rod indicated they should turn back.

At one point on their return the two found themselves in a circling school of tiny fish, vivid darting bodies against a stunning blue. Vaughan would have been breathtaken except there was a line of air direct to his mouth. As they made their way back to the jetty, he silently thanked Rod's unknown cousin and his gear for this opportunity.

'Mind blowing! Stunning! Wicked!' Mere words could not describe what Vaughan felt. Rod was pleased at his young friend's reaction but then, sitting on the jetty, he suddenly seemed nervous, glancing about as if expecting someone.

'Some shipwrecks out there too. We might do them another afternoon,' he told Vaughan as they stacked the gear. Then Rod had taken off leaving Vaughan to trail home alone.

Yet next day he called for Vaughan again. 'I'll show you the Magic Arc, mate. It's a break in the coral reef where the fish congregate. Bloody amazing!' They skimmed over more shallow shelves with large coral heads. Vaughan had never seen such a profusion of colours as mounts of white coral and dancing white grasses gave way to pink and purple, to orange and red and then to the dramatic purplish black of a spongy-looking seaweed. Vaughan felt he never wanted to surface but push on further and further to new discoveries.

I was a fish in another life, must have been, he thought when Rod finally had to motion him upwards and he'd returned unwillingly to the jetty. Here the easygoing Rod was once again anxious, collecting, checking the gear and moving away swiftly, mindful of the boats that came in here on occasions or other younger eyes that might catch sight of them. And so it was every day.

Vaughan hated that time. Stripping himself of the suit as quickly as his cold, unwilling fingers would allow, watching Rod's anxious face and trying to respond to his half-hearted, 'Get a move on, mate!' as he scanned the horizon.

No one ever came by Lonely Place, but the tension of the return to the jetty made Vaughan feel very much the interloper again. It always spoilt the freshness and wonder of the diving.

'See ya,' and Rod was darting away from him without so much as a backward glance. Up the sandhills, leaving a fresh trail of footprints which were already being obliterated as Vaughan followed, making his slow way back home, wondering why Rod's training him had to be such a damned big secret.

But at night he was soaring—yeah—that was the feeling—if you can soar through water? He'd write a letter soon to his dad about it, trying to catch just a bit of it on paper if he could. He wondered if he could describe the intense depth running beside the magic shelf of multi-coloured corals, the dancing schools of vibrant fish scooting past, the languorous play of weed, the outrageous variety of the coral clumps, the gliding, soaring, flying past all of it—one of them and at home. That feeling was so good that for long moments he forgot this was part of his training. Forgot the horror of the cave to come, the persistent nagging worry of the dive.

It was the best possible training, as Rod well knew. An affinity with fish. A love of the water world. Any fear of the underwater evaporated here as the two boys pushed out further and further along the coral reef that circled the Settlement.

Soon Vaughan took to underwater swimming without the gear. 'It's easier than swimming on the surface,' he laughed as Rod timed him in the blue green waters of Madshark Cove. Rod always seemed relaxed here, greeting the others if they came, as they sometimes did, to surf. Each day Vaughan seemed to go a little further, pushing himself to get that word of praise from Rod, which meant he was nearer to his goal. But there came a day when there was no improvement on the day before and he was still far short of the distance.

'Not to worry,' Rod had encouraged. 'Let out your breath slow, slow, slow, like this,' and Rod would do his underwater stint effortlessly and chant the same words, mantra-like for him. But as the days went on, it seemed Vaughan might have reached his maximum capacity as he continued to clock on far short of the dive distance.

'Tell me about Liam then. What's he like?' The day before, Vaughan had to come face to face with Liam at the bread shop. He hadn't known whether he should greet the big boy, whether he'd be ignored. But Liam had given a kind of smile as he passed and Vaughan had walked on home elated.

At Madshark, Rod and he would always lie on the hard sand after their daily exertions in the water, close to the lapping waves to rest and to dry. But Rod wouldn't disclose too much about the leader of the group except to say he had no parents and a young brother who'd died a few years ago, and to end curtly, 'Best friend a mate could ever have.'

Vaughan felt he no longer had to hide and spy on the group of boys as they went through their ritual dive. He'd be one of them soon, he was sure. When they were engaged there, he did a secret training of his own at the beach with no watch to check his time.

And then came the day when Rod called, 'A marked improvement, mate. You're just about ready!

'I'm going to describe the cave tunnel for you. I know every metre of that rock. You better know about the real narrow part—bit of a squeeze!' He drew the shape of the underwater trail in wet sand with his finger. 'Mouth is just that and you're into the Devil's Gullet straight off. Then there's the Shark Pool—no don't worry, no sharks, it's just the shape of a whopper. We call this next bit the Waist and you have to go sideways through it like this. It's high but not wide and Liam and I can't get through easily any more.'

'Why?' Vaughan felt a thrill of fear at this.

'Can't fit,' Rod flexed the muscles of his arms and chest. 'See, your shoulders gotta be no wider than this,' and he held his hands apart indicating a distance.

'You'll be fine,' he said, regarding Vaughan's girth, making him feel weedy.

'It widens out to the place we call the Cathedral. Suddenly there's light and it's very pretty in there. That's where you get the chance to breathe, to say your prayers,' and he smiled. 'At low tide, that is. You never make the dive unless it's low tide, though it's rumoured that Liam's father did. He's dead now so we can't ask, but they said he could do it. Must've had a pair of lungs on him. Don't know that I believe it but that's the story Liam tells. And the kids are very impressed!

'So the Cathedral's a big relief—light and air,' Rod went on. 'You gotta know where to find the air pocket but I'll tell you that later. There's only one thing wrong with the place. You take a big new deep breath,' and he mimed the action, his chest filling, so large and powerful that Vaughan thought he could never, never be like that. 'After that you've got to get your shoulders through the out tunnel and then you're in the Plunge Hole. God, that place seems so dark and the water creepy cold as you go down. It leads down before it goes up and you've got to keep pushing on. It's not that far but that's the part where you think you're going to die.

'Then there's a twist of rock. You coil around that soon as you see the first light, and then swim up and up through masses of light blinding you and fish and green stuff. You're too near bursting to take it all in then you explode into that light again. And finally you reach the Golden Gate—a kind of greeny-gold dazzle with a bit of an arch on it—and you're out! The pool at the end we call Victory Pond. You're just bloody glad to be alive when you get there!'

'Sounds great,' Vaughan said doubtfully, looking at the long, long tunnel Rod had etched in the sand. His heart was sinking at the idea of so many places to pass through to get out the other side.

'Not as far as it looks. Piece of cake once you get the breathing right,' Rod encouraged.

'Sure.'

'But gotta warn you—the worst of it the first time is the dark. See, not far from the mouth of the tunnel it gets real dark. Seaweed curtain closes off the light. Dark for quite a way then there's the patches of light. Keeps you cheerful. You just keep moving. And then a flood of it. And that's when you know you'll be fine!'

'Has anyone ever—you know—anyone ever not made it?'

Rod got up abruptly at this and darted up the beach. 'C'mon, better get cracking. Johnson's dad's wanting help with the haul round now. Wanna come?'

So Vaughan didn't know if anyone had failed, if anyone had ever tried the dive and the swim through the rock tunnel, fought the water and failed the test. Drowned in one of those spots they'd named—the Cathedral, or been caught for horrifying minutes of expelling breath at the Waist or in the Shark Pool. Not made the Victory Pond at all. Rod wasn't prepared to say.

In a recurring nightmare Vaughan saw an image forming of a face. Not an image he welcomed because it came by way of his wretched tunnel dreaming. There was the usual wild underwater struggle and the predatory thing waiting for him but this time flashes of phosphorescence signalled its writhing approach. He put up his arm to ward off the deadly embrace when he could clearly see the underside of those flailing tentacles and the several hundred sucking mouths with hungry, rubbery lips. He found an implement in his hand, a blade, and he didn't hesitate to use it, hacking at the arms wildly. Gelatinous hunks flew round him secreting vomitous froth but the body of the thing, the huge looming blob of gristle, could not be stopped. He felt its irresistible suction and himself being drawn into it, his breath sucked away. Then he was face to face with the murky remnants of its ingestion. And amid dark entrails, a face began to form.

A face whose dark-coloured hair floated out like a seaweed crown round a white, unrecognisable visage. There was a trail of blood floating from the mouth and nose. It woke him, this monster dream that had produced such a haunting, featureless image of someone he strained hard to recognise, the shock of it bringing a sharp nausea. He had to leave his bed the first time it happened.

The wind seemed to be rocking the timbers of the house and spitting sand against the glass and he put his head out the window into the air. Keeping quiet as he could, shoving the window up, so that January wouldn't hear him. Frightened he might chuck out the window. But he didn't and the white face and the grisly monster thing faded as he tasted the sand and his nausea died.

He dreamed of another kind of dive, nights later. Vaughan Jasper Roberts the Third making the dive. And this one a flawless feat, strong swimming movements through a golden tunnel, a smile still on his face as he awoke. Sometimes he dreamed of this by day in the blistering wind among the tussocks where he spent lonely hours away from the house and his grandmother. He knew he had to do it soon, soon, or lose the chance this summer. Lose his nerve.

FOUR

Dear Vaughan,

This is a hard decision for your mother and me to make. We need to do things that don't include having a kid with us at the moment. You know how your mother has dreamed of following her stage career? Well son, we have a chance in LA, both of us, doing an act with an agency there. It's a kind of circuit thing that will take us all over the country and to places not suitable for kids. When we get settled we've told your grandmother we'll send for you.

Your mother asked me to write because just now she's really busy getting costumes made, in rehearsal and all kinds of things and you know how she hates to sit down quietly at any time. We know that you will understand that this is her big opportunity.

I'll be writing to your grandmother but you can tell her about this letter.

I hope you're enjoying the surf and the fishing and have met some new friends. And thanks for your last letter, we enjoyed it and will have an address for you real soon.

With love
Jasper your Dad

Yes, he was enjoying the surfing. And the dives with Rod. Sure he was. He'd met some of the Settlement boys now. He'd like to tell his dad about Liam, the much admired leader, who seemed so distant yet so admirable with his powerful body and his mocking eyes. And Tom and Dyson, Chuck and Paul who were friendly when the mood took them, in a jokey sort of way. Or who would come and surf with Rod and him at Madshark occasionally. But he felt angry about the 'circuit thing'. About being dumped again. And there was nowhere to write to his mum and dad now—not that he could ever seem to find a way to tell them how he really felt. He'd joked around in the last letter, hoping he'd make them laugh, hoping they'd sense his longing for them. Hoping.

But mostly he was sure they simply didn't want to know.

Telling them about the dive might change things—link them, interest them, even worry them just a little. He imagined the letter describing this miraculous undertaking—his father would be sure to know just where and be amazed by such a feat. Maybe his father had made the dive all those years ago and, knowing something about the mystery of the place, would understand Liam's attachment to it.

He was pretty close to doing the dive, he'd tell his parents. He'd memorised each of the hallways and chambers of the volcanic passageway Rod had so brilliantly described for him. He'd etched its parts in the sand when he was alone, as he was so often. He'd draw it for them and he'd tell them the effort he was putting into maintaining his underwater times. He would say he was very, very close.

When he'd asked though, Rod had said, 'Time enough,' as he took off to find Liam and the gang. 'You and I better have a practice run first, before you do it for them. You'll do it okay. No worries! Piece of cake!'

But in reality, when he stood by the gaping mouth of the cave, Vaughan still felt weak with the knowledge of the long, worming tunnel so far under the water. To hell with boasting to his dad or anyone else, he'd think then, it would *not* be a pushover. His feelings waxed and waned, his dreams adding eerie edges to his resolve.

If Rod were with him at the cave, he'd encourage Vaughan in his friendly way. 'You're already nearly doing the time. There's no current like that down there to hold you back. You'll do it flying and no worries. And then you're in!' And Vaughan would feel good for the moment, assured by Rod's confidence.

But in his heart he knew he'd rather be scuba diving, not proving himself down there in black water. No, he'd rather be joining his parents, be with them and their 'big opportunities' that he knew well enough would dwindle to nothing again. He'd write and tell them that his grandmother didn't want him here. He'd insist they send for him. But where in the hell were they right now, anyway?

Letters with no return addresses began to arrive.

Dear Vaughan

We're on a truckstop. Been travelling now so long every bone in my body aches. Going through this desert countryside and I thought since I'm trapped in this motel a few days—a broken axle—I'd write to you.

Your father was dead keen to go on this tour. You know with his drinking how it's been hard to get a job, and then this chance came up. It's a really big chance for him—or that's how he sees it. Well, it's not much of a chance really, a few gigs in God-forsaken holes but because its America he thinks he's made it big. Never mind, your Aunt Meryl paid his fare here in the first place.

Big mistake boy, but we've got a contract and we've got to ride it out. And ride and ride and ride. We travel with a band, half of them real space cadets and your dad not bad competition. He's off the whisky now, thank God, as it makes him mean as mud, but doing speed and says he'll come off once we finish. And then I'll tell him I want to come home. I'm going home come what may.

I think of you there in your father's house. I know January isn't the be all and end of all of a grandmother. She puts a bit of alcohol away too. But she's pretty straight I reckon and you know, sometimes, tearing down these endless hot roads on the way to nowhere, I think of her house. Big and open and beautiful in the way country seaside houses can be beautiful. Your father's room with the cream painted wide boards and the varnished picture rail, tucked back out of the wind of the bay. And the creaky old verandah with the broken down lattice.

I can remember creeping down that verandah and the exact spot where the worst board is located—near the wisteria vine. Your dad and I used to break up into fits of laughter—silent laughter—we didn't want to be caught out by his ma or his pa.

When I think of this I'd like to be there with you looking out onto the water and those queer rock formations all around. I used to know them so well I stopped noticing them. But then when you came along and we went visiting Grandma you cried out in fright the first time you saw them.

We took you over to a friend's place and there was this great rock in the front yard with a little white picket fence around it. Jasper was sure you'd want to climb up on it like he had, but when he lifted you up, boy you hollered. Made your father laugh. You were just a little kid and probably don't remember.

The house was not as she remembered it! He'd been shocked by the down-at-heel appearance of the place the day the Co-op truck had dumped him in the middle of the town. And there was the house to come!

'Can't take you all the way out there, mate. But it's the old grey decrepit number.' The driver had pointed to some tussocky sandhills at the edge of the township where Vaughan glimpsed breaks of blue, blue sea. 'Weatherboard, end of the line.' Seeing the crestfallen young face, the man had seen fit to add, 'Near a bloody good surfing beach but—'

Vaughan had walked through the blistering heat and left the hot little town for the sandy road that led for sure 'to the end of the line'.

'I walk the line,' he sang in his mind along with his father Jasper. 'Because you're mine!' But no, he shouldn't think about Dad or Mum or their endless repertoire of songs. He passed a few houses that could well be described as 'old grey decrepit numbers' but when he finally arrived, his backpack of possessions digging into his shoulders, his shirt wringing wet in the heat, he thought his grand-mother's house would have to take the prize.

A big weatherboard house, yes. But the metal front gate had rusted on the path where it had fallen and a profusion of weeds allowed only a narrow track to the front door. He could see at a glance that lots of windows were broken and as he approached the bleached front door, he noticed that the boards were rotted through on the verandah floor. 'Deluxe!' he wanted to say, the way his dad would have, the way he did when they stopped at yet another run-down old motel.

Later, his grandmother, January Roberts, explained that you came and went by the back door. 'Floor out front's dangerous and with no man around the house...' and she'd glared at him. Was this supposed to be a hint or what? Even in her greeting to him, the cursory hug and the absent-minded peck of a kiss, he'd sensed her unwillingness to have him there, but she did her duty by him. 'Welcome to the Settlement, Vaughan,' she'd managed to say.

All along the ramshackle sides of the house he saw that boards had gone missing and had never been replaced. She'd tacked plastic garbage bags here and there, his grandmother. Bright orange, to cover the holes. Some had escaped her thumb-tacking efforts and flapped and rustled in the wind, adding to the crazy and decrepit appearance of the house. It seemed a house devoured by time and the wind, seemed to be leaning against the wind in fact.

'Best room in the place,' his grandmother had announced taking him into his bedroom.

'Big house to keep clean,' his grandmother observed, leaving him stranded to make his own explorations. He hated the amber glow of the room and his first job was to replace the bright orange 'mended' window panes with clear plastic he'd found in the overstuffed kitchen drawers. January made no comment about it and he was tempted to do the same throughout the house but didn't like to take such liberties. Maybe later, he thought, but then, I won't be here later. He wondered why she'd let things slide like this but didn't have the heart to ask.

Still, the wide verandahs were intact at the back, though the lattice had long since rotted away or been carried by fists of wisteria vine to strange locations, up on the guttering or down round the house stumps. And sometimes, when he sat out there in the whingeing metal chair with its broken ribbing, he could picture his mum and dad creeping along the verandah, hand in hand, laughing...And then he'd remember he was stuck here. And that would make him think about the gang and Liam and the dive.

'Where's that boy got to?' He could hear his grandmother coming up the hall and had the desire to leap away and go hide in the sandhills, something he'd soon learnt was a way out. But before he could move, the impossible wire door, so full of tears it was useless against the swarms of midday flies that buzzed through the house, opened with a whine.

'The Pastor was asking after you again, Vaughan. You should come to the prayer meeting this Thursday. More of the younger people are attending—he's that pleased about it. You've only been once. He thinks it'll go a long way to helping you fit in here. He says he knows all too well what it is to be a stranger. Such a sympathetic man. If only you'd let him be…'

But Vaughan shook his head never mind how she frowned at him. 'You have plans Thursday night, do you?' she asked testily. She'd clattered his plate on the table at dinner that night.

He'd better distract her. Talk about the past she seemed to prefer to the present. 'Why's it called the Settlement?' he asked her.

'Soldier's Settlement,' January told him. 'They gave your grandfather and a whole lot of others a bit of land here after the war. To make a go of farming. A kind of reward that turned out a real trial. What a joke! The soil too sandy, too salty. So they took to the water when they knew the land had beaten them. Learned how to become fishermen. Did well, too, for a lot of years. Before the trouble spoiled all that.'

'The trouble?' He wondered whether it was another war he didn't know about.

'Fish stopped running. Business went bad.'

'Why?'

She shrugged. 'It happens.' She'd look up at her husband's photograph on the wall above them and he saw her expression soften.

'He was a lovely man was Percy. A lovely man. He and his mates built this house with their own hands, you know.' And she looked around with satisfaction at the ancient kitchen cupboards with their dull red, knife-scratched laminex tops, at the pockmarked linoleum and up at the fly-spotted wooden ceiling, as if she were looking at a palace of sorts. 'That's why I could never leave here. Never.' But when she came back to the present her voice hardened.

'Your dad, Jasper, he's not like his father was. That's for sure. Don't know where he came from that Jasper, with his careless, selfish ways. Now his father...' and again she looked back towards the picture of a handsome man, brown eyes with dark curly hair, a face so uncannily like his dad's. 'He was a real man!'

'So is Dad!' Vaughan wanted to say but the thought of his father drunk and abusive suddenly rose up and a real pang went through him and he choked on the words.

■

Outside, the night was restless again and, in his bed, Vaughan was restless too. Images of cascading golden leaves, his mother's hair. Outside the hiss and spittle of a mean rain, hard twigs and worn-out leaves pelting against the water tank, the dry yearning weatherboards of the verandah. Fitful sleep and a morass of unwelcome images. His dad clutching a bottle, eyes bloodshot and mouth big with yelling. The church window cartwheeling and the Pastor's elongated face.

The second time he woke he sat up listening, listening. There was only the ceaseless movement of the sand out there. But somehow it seemed predatory tonight. Out along the humped hills, cascading rills of it and the larger waterfalls of the fine moving stuff stirring, being stirred in the willy-willy that would pass through here. Never a refreshing wind, but one that was gritty and rasping at the windows, he thought, throwing the damp-smelling doona off. The plastic over the windows rustled. He lay back exhausted. A sharp image of Liam's long hard stare. His unfathomable stare. Then a lapse into a black hole of sleep—the Plunge Hole Rod had described for him, where weedy arms seemed to always drag him down and down…

He thought of the Pastor's face on waking and pushed the unwelcome image away. And in the morning, listening to the ascending scale of the wind as he ate breakfast, he decided that he definitely *would not* go back to the church again. Whatever she said. It would mean long explanations to his grandmother but better that than the dim church interior where he'd felt scrutinised to the bone. Where he'd felt like one of those insects trapped in an ambery liquid forever. Worse still the Pastor's hoary breath when he embraced each of them on leaving the place, and his hand too much on his arm. The force of his friendship that was in no way real friendship.

'He saved me, the Pastor did. Saved me from the bottle

and despair!' his grandmother declared at another of her breakfast exhortations. She saw him glance at the line of bottles by the tidy bin in the kitchen.

'Of course, Vaughan, I'm not saying I don't still take a drink now or then. But before the Pastor, before him, I was—I was at the mercy of the demons before he came here. That's what he said I was! And he sent the demons running.'

'How?'

'He laid his hand on my head and he prayed for me. He came here and did that. He said that was necessary. Imagine, right into the kitchen that man came, so we could pray together. It was the strangest, most wonderful thing.' She dabbed at her eyes with the corner of her worn apron. 'I felt like Percy had come back home and I told the Pastor so. Like the house had come back to life again. He was so pleased when I said that.

'And then we prayed in the church with seven witnesses. That's what we needed, he said, to get rid of my demons. Seven's a holy number you see. And I had to find them. Took me a few weeks to talk the folk round here to coming. But I did, over and over. And they came, my old friends who've been missing the church. They came, seven of them.'

'But with you and the Pastor wouldn't that make nine?'

'Oh Vaughan, you say the silliest things. Seven witnesses. And now they all go regular-like to his church. Them and their families. Lots of them gone into the Compound too.' She ignored his frown as she shoved cold toast toward him.

'It's a real rebirth of belief round here. Wonderful! He talks a lot about rebirth, you know. But that's secret and you can't really know about that unless you join in. I'm sure you will.'

He hadn't heard her so animated. She'd obviously been quite changed in the past weeks since the Pastor had 'saved' her—he wasn't sure from what.

'And he gave me this. Has to be with me at all times. Well, it doesn't really—I mean he didn't say so—but it makes me feel safe and protected you know.'

It was an ugly thing. A talisman, harmless-looking, carved of coral perhaps. Familiar but why should it be? Then he remembered. He'd seen some of the townspeople wearing one like it. He'd seen Liam!

'Oh,' was all he could think to say.

'The demons are gone now, thanks to the Master!' she told him.

He thought she was speaking metaphorically when she'd mentioned her demons, but she'd looked behind her as she spoke to him, as if fearful they'd leap out of the broom cupboard or hop over the sagging window sills.

'So you'll have to come to church too, Vaughan. I want that! He said in particular, in the prayers, that he wants that too.' She was shovelling great lumps of half-melted butter thickly onto her toast. Eating noisily and he felt repulsed. She didn't say, I'd like that or maybe you'd like to come. *I want that. He wants that, too.*

He said nothing. She rose and he felt that she was automatically making for the cupboard where the alcohol was stored. He'd seen her stash. But she swerved away, feeling his eyes on her.

'Now you can go and do the shopping for me,' her voice

had a different tone, and he knew she was getting rid of him. He was glad to go.

Oh this is fun, Vaughan thought as he trudged through the sandy main street again. Such rip-roaring fun!

The deadening atmosphere of the town hit him again. He was in a tropical town—there should be vibrancy to equate with the bursts of scarlet bougainvillea and double pink shocks of hibiscus along the way. But he felt hostile eyes regarding him from dim interiors and sullen tones greeted him in the shops he was forced to visit. There was a weightiness in the air like the weight of heat, he thought, but a deadly weight, as if the sun were scowling at their ant-like antics here on their pathetic tracks to and from the town to the unyielding sea.

'January quite well?' the languid-looking baker placed the loaf in a bag, already greasy at the touch of her finger-tips. It was as if he were the cause of some possible ill health, Vaughan thought.

'Miss January is sure running up a meat bill these days,' the butcher commented as Vaughan took the package of sausages from him. The idiot should be pleased for his grandmother's custom, that she wasn't vegetarian, Vaughan thought as he made his way through the heat. He hated coming into this shop which now, like some of the others, sported a picture of the Pastor. It sat, bright and fierce in its colouring, above the faded, fly-dunged poster claiming 'Best Cuts of Lamb'.

Vaughan walked back past the co-op fish shop with its bleached shutters banging heedlessly in the wind. Okay, the town was going bust. Well, why the hell didn't they change their line of business.? Quit fishing and go into net-making for the towns doing it big. Or go into the tourist trade, he thought with youthful reasoning. Mind you, they'd all have to do a hospitality course. Yes, a few smiles and friendly service from those left in the town wouldn't go amiss round here.

Darling Vaughan.

The service in America is amazing. We're in Hollywood, Vaughan, and we've thought of you so many times.

We're staying at a place where all the stars stayed. Marilyn Monro, Grace Kelly—all the golden years people. You wouldn't believe it.

The hotel is called Chateau Marmont and it's based on a French chateau built in the thirties. But hang onto your hat love, we're not paying—well, not directly.

We're really on an up at last! House of Blues just down the road are giving me a season. It's unbelievable stuff. Your father's drinking far less now and he's bought some decent clothes for a change

I must say when I signed the contract (unfortunately they don't want him as guitarist but that's another story) we headed straight for Rodeo Drive. My kind of street—all the big label places and shops to die for. And I bought you a shirt, darling. Oranges and lemons all over it and bright as anything—very in at the moment. It cost a bomb of course and should set old Jan's eyes rolling. Don't tell her I said that and yes, yes we're sending her some money—soon—next cheque, darling. We did such a spend up. Both a bit delirious I guess!

And in the shops, Vaughan, in the shops here, it's yes ma'am and no ma'am and three bags full ma'am. And have a nice day. Makes a nice change to See Ya!

Your father just heard that Grace Kelly used to roam the corridors of this hotel at night wearing long black gloves, and that Howard Hughes—an eccentric millionaire—used to stay here for months on end. They say he had a spyglass on his verandah and he'd spy on the little starlets frolicking in the pool down below his penthouse and he'd just point out the one he wanted.

So Hollywood, huh? Your dad says hi and he's going to be roaming the corridors tonight himself! Not really but you should see him smoking cigars down by the pool. It just seems to come natural to him, this millionaire stuff.

He's that happy at the moment.

Vaughan felt angry. He felt like crying. He didn't need a shirt. He didn't need to hear how Hollywood their lives were becoming. He needed an escape route. She was settled in big time, his mother. And so was his dad. They wouldn't come home for a long time now.

FIVE

'The Pastor's coming, that's what!' As he swept he could hear the panic in her voice, hear the cold clink of so many bottles being stashed determinedly out of sight. 'That's why I'm telling you to smarten up! You're going to be a useless dreamer like your dad if you don't watch out. Now get going!'

He moved the broom faster then. 'Bloody sand,' he thought as particles flew up before the straw broom and subsided on the cracked linoleum again. 'Fights it way back in here, no matter what!'

'Hurry along with that!' He was brushing the heaped sand into the dustpan as she passed by again.

'You could give the candlesticks a good going over with the Brasso then. And don't look at me like that. It's only a small thing to ask you!'

She was on the run from bathroom to bedroom, a

quivering coxcomb of rollers in her hair. 'Look in the corners—there and there! Trouble is you're just not used to hard work. All you young people are the same. You need discipline, that's what the Pastor reckons and I think he's right.'

What was the use of talking to her? he thought, rubbing the twists of the rust-spotted candelabra that had been sold to his grandmother, she'd said, when the Catholic church quit the Settlement altogether. The church building had quickly gone into decay. Until the Pastor had come to town and claimed it as his own.

'A resurrection,' some of the townspeople had first joked seeing the activity up there. Suddenly the windows were unboarded, broken walls were mended, sand swept away and the doors opened again. The tight-knit group of his followers worked tirelessly with the Pastor to raise the new sign *Church of the Most Cherished Spirits*, to the sky. And some of the townspeople gave him grudging admiration. 'He's a real goer. Got to give him that much. And he's getting some of those lazy bums round here working!'

And a lot more than that, Vaughan thought, as he saw them trickle by on Sunday to the new church with its new ways, its modern music and the Pastor's enticing sermons. 'He gets out and about in the community too,' his grandmother had said admiringly. 'That's why people like him—he's so personal is the Pastor!' Vaughan rubbed the candelabra with venom. Even the shine on the gold seemed dull and salt-smeared here. Maybe the salt and sand preyed on your very soul. But it won't be you, Old Pastor Blue Eyes, who tries to save mine,' he determined.

She'd definitely changed over the last few weeks, his

grandmother. Instead of sitting around as she'd first done when he'd arrived, she seemed nervously busy all of the time and keen on keeping him busy too. She'd combed her hair in a new way and put makeup on. She'd looked out the door several times and then rushed to the mirror when the emerald car began making its way down the lonely hill that led to their house. Vaughan saw the Pastor kiss his grandmother on the lips and put his hand lower than her waist when he put one arm around her, embracing her. His eyes were cold, fathomless as the sea, and yet Vaughan felt they sought something. He shifted uneasily in his presence.

'Let us meditate together, friends,' the Pastor intoned. His grandmother had placed a drooping hibiscus on the table in front of him.

'You can close your eyes too, Vaughan, and just relax,' she told him.

In the quiet he heard it again—the incessant wind grinding its teeth. Particles were already working their way under the door where he'd just swept. He could almost taste them in his mouth. Bugger it!

The sound of the ever present sea was like a dull suction today, drawing the energy and will from him. A fly buzzed infuriatingly at the window and he could have jumped up and made a kung fu move and killed the thing, sent the already broken glass flying too. But instead he closed his eyes and rested his head on the flock lounge seat. The fly seemed to take this as a signal and subsided. Now the Pastor was mumbling away. It was a bristly feel at his neck but it was easy to give in to those words just now, and go with them—just go.

Vaughan's eyes flew open as a scaly hand pressed hotly

over his. His grandmother and the Pastor, eyes still closed, had joined hands, their faces intent in their supplication. How could he extricate himself from the hands and the inevitable entry into the Pastor's flock? He felt he was on shifting sand with nowhere to turn. Well, he'd just go along with it for now but he was no sheep to follow on like so many others had.

'Oh Heavenly and Most Cherished Masters, Great and Mighty Powers of the most Divine Universe revealed to us alone, guide me now. Let us know where we will find the One. Admit January's blood, her kith and kin to this most Cherished and Divine Circle that his Purpose here may be divined.'

Silence again—the wind's sigh and moan, a boy's cry way off and the slap of wave after wave. The fly started up again, its body beating uselessly against the window pane.

'Thank you dear ones,' and the hand, thank God, was removed from his. His grandmother and the Pastor looked at one another.

'Pastor? she asked.

He shook his head and frowned. 'Not yet, no not yet.'

Good, that let him off the hook, whatever they were talking about. No church for him tomorrow.

'Get the tea tray, Vaughan.' Gladly he left them to their tea to walk across sandhills towards the apron of hot volcanic rock. Maybe they were having it off—the pair of them. She was certainly fussing over him like a lover, like his mother fussed over his dad when she wanted a favour. Or maybe it was a trick the Pastor played, making all the women—the middle aged and the elderly following that he was getting, more of the community each day they said—think that he adored them.

'Do you believe as I do, my boy?' the Pastor had asked in that infuriating paternalistic way of his the one time Vaughan had gone to the church. 'Do you have it in your heart to acknowledge that you've been called to this place? Called to the Settlement?'

'Called?' Dumped more like it.

'The sea called me here,' the Pastor explained. 'The Divine Ones used the sea to call me, to explain my purpose. I heard it and I know it plain as day. I've offered myself to serve this community, here by the sea that is failing them, as it was deemed right and proper I should do.'

'My mum and dad have no other relatives, there's nowhere else for me to go this summer. That's why I'm here,' Vaughan said stubbornly, staring out the door of the church at the curve of rock and the slice of sand.

'Which amounts to the same thing, don't you see? Your destiny decided for you. Paths cross, my boy, for a purpose, I know that. And I know it's not always clear why. But if you acknowledge that and allow the Cherished Spirits to enter your soul, purpose will be revealed to you. You must join your grandmother, for her sake and indeed and most importantly, my boy, for your own.'

There had seemed just the slightest hint of threat in his voice. Vaughan hated being called 'my boy' like that. 'I don't go in for that stuff. My mum and dad are agnostics and so am I!' he'd said and saw the flash of anger in the man's eyes. Vaughan left as quickly as he could.

Purpose! He knew the reason he was here was divined by mere mortals. His parents were absolving themselves of responsibility via the post. He recognised that as the letters got longer and more loving, the chance of being reunited soon was becoming all the more remote. The continued absence of any forwarding address made it impossible to tell them what he was feeling.

Vaughan left the smooth sand and headed directly to the punishing rock surface. He kicked at the rock. Already over these past few summery weeks his feet had toughened. He was momentarily pleased. He was toughening up as Rod said he would. He could run as well as the other boys, he knew that, and he'd swim as well soon enough.

He walked over the rocks, not without care where the spikes were less worn down, towards their place. The gang's. There was not a boy in sight, just two gulls hovering about at the water's edge. One hopped on its single leg and he wondered how it survived in a bird-peck-bird world like this. It was the braver of the two, coming closer, hoping for some crumbs. He threw his hands up to show they were empty and the sudden movement startled both the birds into flight. If only he could fly off like that.

He looked down at the swirling cave entrance, practically submerged today by high tide, drawn to it as usual. If anything was his purpose here, if you needed a purpose at all, the discovery of an underwater world, the dives with Rod, must be it. And the initiation dive. Forget his parents for the moment, that's what he should do. Resist the bloody Pastor and his caterwauling and make every effort to join the lads here. Make the dive and enter into the kind of real fellowship he wanted—to be with Rod and Liam and the others, to be one of them. He wanted more than anything else to be allowed to run wild with them. Swim and dive

with them, go on their useless fishing trips, their boy
binges in the sandhills, their cruises through town which
Rod had described, looking for girls. Part of the gang and
part of this God-forsaken place.

He looked away to the surf, crests of white and magic
blue water rolling in at the nearby beach. He should go for
a swim but he didn't make a move. Just sat in the hot sun
on the salt-flecked rocks near the cave. Something was dri-
ving him towards making that dive. But what? A dive that
was tough and would risk his life, all so that he could be
part of their purposeless lives? Why did he want that so
much?

The sea was subsiding and in the hour that he sat there
the pool was smoothing over. He could see the gaping
watery mouth better—the dark hole and the flagellating
curtain and the entrance pool itself. Through the calmer
ripples of water he could see patches of yellow sand and
dark rock at the bottom. He craned to look at the chequer
board it made and saw something else. He stood up to
view it better. There was something there weighted down
by pebbles. Seemed to be something not sea made. He
stripped and dived into the pool.

All over the sand were small rusty circlets of wire, hundreds of them. He grasped one and brought it up to the
surface. Sitting naked on the rock he examined it, a wire
looped round with a hook and eye to complete the circle.
From one side a claw of finer wires extended and shells had
been attached. Obviously it'd been there a while. He held
it up this way and that in an attempt to make sense of the
shape. Was it the wreath the boys wore momentarily, or

something like it? Perhaps a crude attempt at a sculptured fish?

'I'd put it back if I were you.' How he jumped at that voice! Stark naked as he was, found fishing in their precious part of the world. He dropped the circlet and grabbed his shorts. She didn't drop her gaze as he dressed.

'—where it belongs,' she insisted and she stooped to pick it up where it had fallen.

'What the hell is it?' he asked

'None of your business is what it is...' She picked up a pebble and deftly, as if she'd done it many times before, fitted it inside a loop of the finer wire. A weight of course. He watched her, a young girl in faded shorts and shirt, a simple coral necklace at her throat.

She dropped the circlet back in the pond. 'Where it belongs,' she said emphatically, but again with that blank and humourless expression.

'There are so many of them down there. I'm just curious—'

'You know what curiosity did?' And now there was the ghost of a smile as she turned. She was already leaping up the rocks as sure-footed as any of the boys. 'Not your territory here and you know it!' she called back down to him

'And not yours!' he challenged and then on impulse he added, 'I could tell them about your visit here! Liam and the gang!' He didn't know why he'd said it and he didn't dream of its impact.

She came back down beside him in a minute. 'No, don't do that please, don't say I've been here. It'd cause all sorts of trouble.'

She was worried, that was clear. Well, at least he'd had

some sort of reaction. He was powerful for a moment. He plunged on.

'Then tell me. If you tell me I won't—' She nodded her head. 'What's your name?'

'Nona—it's Aboriginal for girl.'

'Vaughan. Vaughan Roberts.'

'Hullo, Vaughan Roberts. I can't tell you much.'

'Well, shall I say that you dropped by this afternoon and that we chatted together?'

Her eyes blazed, her colour mounted. 'Okay, you've got me. They're tributes for someone, if you must know...'

'Hey c'mon, you can do better than that!'

'For someone called Benny,' she spat the name at him. 'He's dead. And I'm not saying another word and you're not to.'

'Okay, okay, but stay just a moment.' Already she had turned away again. He thought she was very pretty with her lustrous dark hair and flashing eyes.

'Can't,' she called back when she'd reached the top of the rock but there was a different note in her voice this time. He felt that in some way they had connected.

SIX

There was no one on the beach. A working bee and a bar-
becue at the Compound had taken all the boys away this
afternoon. All, it seemed, but Rod and Vaughan. The
younger boy was following the older, a great seal of a
figure, his largish form always so graceful in the water. Just
watching him now Vaughan knew his underwater prowess
would never match Rod's. He seemed to have an almost
Olympian capacity.

'Gotta get going soon,' Rod called out. 'Their barbie will
be finished and some of us are meeting at the usual place.
C'mon then, let's see ya dive!'

Vaughan swam parallel to the shore, determined he'd
see stars before he'd surface. But the hungry longing for
air sent him upwards long before the desired time, he was
sure.

'Hey mate, mate, you made it that time!' Rod was

checking his watch, excited. 'A couple over, I reckon!' His voice was admiring and he splashed playfully at Vaughan. 'You're ready, you know that! You're bloody ready, Vaughan Roberts!'

'I'd rather be scuba diving,' Vaughan joked but he was pleased he'd at last made the time. Pleased for Rod, too, for all those hours of training.

When they left the water they both made their way towards the point where they could see some of the group members were gathered. A line of them, boys hugging their knees and surveying the scene, strangely still. Vaughan hung back as usual. He knew he could walk around the huge craggy columns, the ones forced into that towering semi-circle by some angry ancient land disturbance, before Rod would come back. So that's what he did, timing himself with the obsession of a diver.

Maybe Rod would set the date and time for the dive right now. His heart beat heavily at the thought. But then he'd never have to hang back like this. He went from the first stone to the next. He practised holding his breath for longer and longer periods as he tagged the monsters. He could make three of them with comfort. Today, if he'd improved underwater, he'd improve on land as well. He'd make the fourth.

From the highest rock column, still dizzy from his effort, he looked over the sandhills and back towards the town where he could clearly see the other rock columns protruding from time to time. What an eerie landscape. His mother had once described a similar place in England where ancient people had dragged the stones into a huge circle that was still there, studded all the way through the village. But this was Nature's handiwork and just as amazing. He caught sight of the church and looked away, back to where Rod and the boys were still engaged in private conversation.

The gang hardly greeted Rod when he reached them. They stood up in a hard circle not quite letting him in.

'What's up then?' Rod asked them, aware of some awkwardness, some change. He kept his news back, that the newcomer was about to be initiated. There was a sullen silence, Dyson kicking at the rocky outcrops with hard scabby toes.

The others scraped and thudded their heels and toes, avoiding his eyes.

'Liam.' Sandy finally said.

'Look, Liam's a bit down at the moment, but he'll come good,' Rod told them, trying to explain Liam's absence. He knew Liam had somehow got them caught up with the Pastor.

'He's okay, I seen him this morning and this afternoon.' Dyson's green eyes were wide in Liam's defence. 'He said we gotta go to them meetings—and we're going—all of us. You should too. At the church.'

'I'm not going inside that place again. It's not a church any more since Father James went.' Rod was angry.

'It's a church—only it's a new Pastor, that's all.'

'That Pastor! I don't trust him and his promises and neither should you. He's not even a priest. Jamesey was a mumbling old bore of a priest, that's for sure. But he had a message. Be generous spirited. Forgive, all that—'

'Kind of crap,' Dyson finished and the others laughed.

'He's a fake, this new Pastor—that's what I reckon. And

he's pushing a cult thing here with people who are out of luck and out of jobs.'

'Who said?'

'My mother for one,' Rod announced. His mother had taught more than one of them and he knew they respected her. 'All his talk about punishing the rest of the world by locking yourself away from it, she reckons that's crazy talk. Maybe dangerous!' He could see some of the boys, Tom and Sandy, shifting uneasily.

'One of the Nooan boys came there this afternoon,' Sandy offered.

'No kidding?' Rod was surprised. 'Bet he didn't stay.'

'Not long,' Sandy agreed. 'Me mum likes him,' Sandy went on, 'she swears by him.'

'And do you? Can you really say you like him?' Sandy was still wearing the welts of the Pastor's punishment. Beating the devil out, he'd told Sandy's grateful mother.

'Nup, hate his guts I do. But Dyson says, Liam says—'

'Shut up, will you,' Dyson's green eyes flashed in anger. 'Rod knows he can come, or he can piss off. It's up to him. But Liam wants to know about you, Chi. What's it to be?'

'None of your bloody business or his, that's what it's to be. And tell him I said so.'

'He's up at the church. Tell him yourself then.'

Rod turned and climbed angrily back up the spiky rock and for the first time he felt the points of jagged stone intrude into his horny heels. Why was Liam sending messages anyway? Why wasn't he speaking to him directly? Rod hardly noticed Vaughan who'd come down from the stone-henge outcrop to trail behind him silently.

'When am I going to do the dive?'

'Didn't talk about it!' Rod barked, lost in dark thoughts of his own.

Liam would surely see reason when they did talk. Hell, they'd known each other for such a long time. They'd discussed the Pastor's ludicrous plans and his obvious methods of brain-washing only a few weeks back. Liam would laugh, roll his eyes heavenward and spread his arms in the old mocking way and pray to the Divine Imposter as they'd called him that day when they'd left his first service, filled with derision for the others.

'What's up?' Vaughan asked him

'Don't know...but I'm going to the church.' Rod was thoughtful as he paced along the sand. 'They said Liam's up there right now.'

'My grandmother told me lots of kids, lot of people are over at the Compound. They've painted the old pub and she says it's great. And now they're fixing up the huts for more suckers, I reckon.' Vaughan was catching up with Rod's angry stride.

'I know.'

'I wouldn't go up there. No way'

'I want to see what's going on.'

'Walk a crooked mile...' Vaughan said suddenly looking down on the town as they parted company

Rod walked quickly past the first rocky outcrop. Vaughan's crooked mile all right. He'd become used to those blind rocks thrusting upwards all over the town, he and his friend Tom Vee had climbed them many times. But sometimes, like now, they did seem strange intrusions, like some prehistoric monster's tooth. Surely the rock had moved, listed so that it would unseat any climber these days? No, he was just thinking that way this morning. Everything seemed off balance really. His mother had said the town had changed overnight.

'Look at the way Liam's changed. Hasn't come near us since he's been going up there to him! Now why, I'd like to know.'

'His business!' Rod had said tersely.

There was no getting away from it though, he was really missing Liam. The fine tanned face, the laughing blue eyes, the irreverent comments, the devil-may-care attitude. The madness. Why in the hell would Liam go and get caught up with this Pastor character? That was real madness! He'd sort him out and he'd do it right now.

Walking up the hill to the spruced-up church and looking out to the cool blue of the sea, Rod felt a sudden confidence. They'd have a good talk and Liam would explain what was going on.

But the church was locked and obviously empty. He didn't want to go over to the Compound, not really, so he turned for home again.

His mother was right. 'They're bored—must be,' she had commented as first Sunday morning and then Wednesday night and then Thursday morning had seen a stream of people going past their house, to the Pastor's meetings. Then the Cleary women, two sensible community-minded women from next door, had gone to live in the Pastor's house 'to look after the poor man'. For some strange reason the Clearys had stopped talking to his mum. They didn't talk much to anyone who wasn't in the Pastor's pocket.

Then the Beresfords had gone to live in one of the old

fisherman's cottages by the hotel and the sudden improvement in the behaviour of the Beresford kids had been the talk of the town. Impressive enough that Mrs Knott had followed with her unruly brood, and then one family after another. The men, many of them out of work for months if not for years, were all pitching in doing up the place. The hotel and the line of houses and even the old barracks came alive with this new tenancy.

There was always the sound of laughter and good cheer early evening from the Compound when the families came together to sing and prepare communal meals. Perhaps that's what drew some of the straggly and unsatisfactory family groups across the sandhills to the Pastor's domain. But not Rod's mother and not Rod.

'You'd think people would see what he's doing. Hell bent on establishing a cult here which gives all power to one person—the Pastor.'

Rhonda Chi had been quick to tell Rod and Nona and others who would listen that the Pastor had been taught all those techniques he used so adroitly. To get people mixing and then disclosing their troubles, have them feeling good, full of hope for the future but heavily dependent on him, making them ripe over time, for complying. 'It's like a mass hypnotism. I'm sure of that. And it suits some people to be told what to do, what to think.'

Seemed to Rod it suited a lot of people in this town.

'There are courses you can do that use elements of what he says. I've been to some so I know what I'm talking about. But there's one critical difference: they set out to help you think for yourself, make up your own mind!'

Rhonda had called a few meetings among the parents

she knew of the kids who were gathering over in the Compound. The first meeting had been crowded but, over time, the crowd had diminished till only a handful seemed to want to discuss the Pastor these days.

'They'll be the losers in the end when he takes off with their kids or their savings—or when something worse happens. Anyway, it looks like it's reached saturation point.'

But the migration continued and would, Rod thought, until there was no one left outside the wire. 'It's like trying to turn the tide, Mum, getting people up in arms over that man and his methods.'

'Well, I'm not going go along with it.'

'Then take the consequences,' he said. 'Or move out!' He wasn't being smart or aggressive and she knew that.

'I'm looking for a new job,' she told him, 'and I'm writing a very interesting article on the takeover of a small, dying fishing town. But I won't be publishing it until we're well clear of here!'

As he passed by the shops in the town, Rod caught sight of the butcher sluicing down the bloody metal in the window, all the meat removed now. Rod gave a curt wave but the butcher ducked his head and made great wide sweeps in the rosy water. Was he imagining things or was he being avoided?

At the bread shop he called out deliberately, 'Hullo there!' but even young Sophie, who'd always had something to say, who always gave a cheery wave, looked away. And the baker seemed to be dusting the empty shelves, scraps and crusts of bread flying. Sour dough, he thought defensively.

What was this? Why weren't they speaking to him now?

Was it because his family and some of the others had chosen last week at the meeting to stay outside the Compound once and for all? Or was it because they were doing some research on the Pastor's American counterpart church? Surely this didn't mean...He quickened his pace as if expecting something untoward when he got home. Most of the houses were shuttered and empty in his street, so many people had left the town in the last few months, more in the last few weeks. But he saw the comfort of lights at the end of the road and his mother's figure moving about the lounge room. He hoped his sister was at home. She'd have seen Liam at the barbeque and he wanted to have a talk to her.

SEVEN

Rod was uneasy as he made his way to Liam's house. He'd had to rely on Nona to learn he might find Liam there. The sun was already high. It seemed the summer had turned around for him altogether. Carefree, golden days and the sheer pleasure of swimming with mates seemed a thing of the past. Yet it had only been a few weeks ago that he and Liam had worked out in great detail a scuba dive adventure beyond the reef. They had planned to explore the wreck out there, just the two of them. His heart felt heavy as he arrived at the beach house which Liam had once shared with his aunt.

Liam's aunt had left the Settlement when her small-goods store finally closed. She didn't like the Pastor or Liam's friendship with him and had said so more than once.

She had packed everything and by the time the truck came to take the last sticks of furniture, Liam was more or less settled in at the Centre, one of the former hotel rooms in the Compound.

Nona had told Rod that she and Liam still met here, at the old house, on occasions. 'The Pastor's not too keen on me and no matter what he says about my being welcome, I feel spooky over there with Liam.'

'That's because it is spooky!' her brother answered.

'Liam,' Rod called tentatively at the open door. Inside there was the feeling of desolation shared by all the houses in these empty streets. 'Liam!' Louder and bolder. In Liam's room there was a mattress, a few candle stubs and one of Liam's summer shirts on a wire hanger. A loud blue one, hanging awry, in a way that only added to the air of desertion. Rod didn't hang around. He was determined to find Liam today.

At the Compound, Rod found Dyson working in the front yard. He was stripped to the waist and despite the heat, was obviously enjoying his task, mixing cement for what looked like a new path to the hotel entrance. Rod hadn't seen Dyson for weeks, not since the day at Devil's Head and something in the boy's self-satisfied manner annoyed him.

'Liam'll be glad to see you here,' Dyson told him, resting on his shovel. 'You decided to come over after all.' Dyson gave such a supercilious smile Rod felt a quick anger.

'I just want to talk to Liam,' he said curtly, 'so where is he?'

'Reckon he's at the church right now.' Dyson turned back to his digging and Rod was about to leave but he was stopped by a disturbing sound.

'What's that?' There was no mistaking a low groan.

Dyson shrugged. 'Pastor's got someone cooling off in there.'

'Where?' The groaning resumed and Dyson knew he couldn't stop Rod investigating. 'Not your business but he's in the laundry, over there. Bit of a drama freak, that Sandy Mason.'

The sound stopped when Rod rattled the handle of the laundry door. It wouldn't open. 'Sandy, that you in there?'

'Yeah.' He heard the muffled voice.

'You better leave him be,' Dyson warned. 'The Pastor's real mad at him.'

'So he locks him up? What is this?' He looked around to where some of the men were working down the way, re-erecting the high barbed-wire fence that had long since fallen down in the wind. 'A bloody concentration camp or what?'

'You better clear off.' Dyson spoke sharply now.

'Not before I hear he's okay. Sandy!' he called, rattling the knob of the door again.

'I'm okay,' Sandy's voice was clearer now. 'Gave the Pastor some cheek this morning. His idea of thinking time. Bloody hot, that's all!'

'They'll let him out of there soon,' Dyson was quick to explain.

'You come and see me then, Sandy. Tomorrow. I want to be sure about this. That you're okay. Or I'll be coming back to check.' This for Dyson and the Pastor as well as Sandy.

'Okay, sure!'

As Rod turned to go something caught his eye through a set of partly opened double doors under the hotel building. A bright blue petrol can. When he looked more closely he saw what seemed like hundreds of them in there and other stores piled high to the roof—crates and tea chests, boxes and bundles and tins. He would have gone inside but Dyson sprang forward to close the doors.

'What's with the petrol?'

'Private property,' Dyson said.

Rod strode though the Compound gates, dark thoughts crowding his mind as he mounted the hill once again where the church, fresh with paint, stood on the rise above the town. What kind of man locked up an ineffectual kid like Sandy Mason? What was Sandy's mum doing about it? What about the other adults there? Why would Dyson, let alone Liam, go along with it? And why in the hell was the man stockpiling stuff? Rod had seen trucks go into the Compound over the last few weeks and now he knew why. Was the Pastor expecting a famine or a war?

The doors of the church stood open. He paused for a moment. It had been months, no years, since Rod had entered this place. He cleared his throat awkwardly and spoke the name. 'Liam!'

It was so dark that it took a moment to make out the altar. The stained-glass windows above had been all but covered by large laminated photographs of the Pastor. As Rod made his way past the line of pews he thought of Father James and the gentle old priest's mumbling voice, of the luminosity of the stained glass that changed during the service as the sun moved round. Rod used to watch it, judging the time of the sermon by its movement. All that seemed an age ago now. He genuflected, and as he crossed himself, wondered why he'd done this so automatically.

'Liam!' he called loudly. 'Anyone here?'

The Pastor not, thank God! Funny he'd thanked a God he no longer thought he believed in. Rod sat in one of the pews and he wished he didn't feel such an emptiness. So much had changed here since the Pastor had taken over. And what he'd seen and heard of the Pastor in the town, what he'd learned today within the Compound only verified his early opinion of the man. It was a suffocating place now with all thoses images of that middle-aged man looking down at him. What in the hell did Liam and so many others see in him?

Rod came out of the dim interior aware of the calming whiteness, the cleanness of the sand down past the town, and the vast blue of the sea that seemed to be sending icy, meandering streams far out to the horizon. A couple of hump-backed whales were spouting out there but today he didn't get the usual thrill of pleasure at seeing them, though he stood and watched until they disappeared from view.

'Rod, hey Rod! Dyson said you were looking for me mate.' And there was Liam coming up the hill, cheerful, friendly, as if not a day had passed.

But their conversation was strained from the beginning. It was Liam and yet it didn't seem to be Liam of old. All he wanted to talk about was the Compound and the Pastor and the way they were changing his life—and the way they could change Rod's.

'Hey, the Pastor said he's going to be needing extra teachers. He's got friends of his coming from the States next month to run the new school. But your mum could take over a teaching role too, in the Compound, if you came.'

Liam, using words like 'role'!

They were passing by the stonehenged rocks. The diving pool, *their* diving pool was only a stone's throw from them. 'You're not coming to Devil's Head any more. Nor are the others.'

'Look mate, we go to Devil's Head mornings mostly, these days. All of the boys who used to go before. And the Pastor's training us.

'What? Not Padi training?' Rod joked, imagining the Pastor leading a group complete with air tanks and scuba diving suits deep into the underwater.

'Nah. It's not a game. It's kind of...well it's an initiation thing. Look, it's hard to explain and I'm not s'posed to talk to—' He saw Rod frown and knew he was avoiding the word 'outsiders'.

'It's a kind of christening so that you're part of the group. Only not a christening, of course. You have to see for yourself. Why don't you give it a go?' He seemed genuinely eager that his friend be part of whatever it was the Pastor was 'initiating'.

But Rod shook his head. To his surprise Liam laughed. 'Still the same old tough nut, eh? There's a kind of price on your head, you know.'

'What?'

'Not like that. Just that the Pastor's said anyone who can convince you or the Roberts kid to come over gets an automatic easy entry into the Inner Circle.'

'Inner Circle? Sound like a kids' club where you get free ice-creams.'

'It's the best. And it's something I definitely can't explain. Well, not right here and now.' They were walking slowly back down the hill, Liam talkative, engaging, Rod feeling more and more morose.

'You should at least give the Pastor a go,' Liam said at last inclining his head in the direction of the Compound. 'You might be surprised.'

'Funny you mentioned Vaughan Roberts before. He's making really good time, that kid. I told him I reckon he could do the dive now.'

'Yeah?' Liam was interested.

'But I'll tell him don't bother to do it on account of the gang. Only to please himself, if he wants to. There isn't a gang any more.'

'There is,' Liam insisted, 'only it's another kind.'

Rod didn't need to say it was one to which he didn't care to belong.

'Be seeing you,' Rod felt defeated.

'Yeah, see ya!' and Liam was off along a different path.

EIGHT

Vaughan was spread-eagled on the sand after his surf,
avoiding January and a list of useless jobs in the house. He
was planning yet another letter to his parents—not strewn
with general complaints—but coming to the point, telling
about what was going on here. For once *really* telling
them, not only about what was happening but how he *felt*
about it. Without the jokes and good cheer. And telling
them why they should, they must, let him join them immediately.

In the last few weeks, the place had gone a bit mad in
its salty, sandy preacher-ish way. Maybe it had gone a lot
mad. More than half of the tiny population of the town had
actually moved out of their plain but perfectly comfortable
homes now. January had commented on it to him in a
pleased sort of voice, hinting that they would probably be
next.

'The Compound's just a hive of activity,' she said. 'It's a pity some of the townsfolk can't see what's happening there. They'd be way less critical if they could. All those meetings trying to drum up bad feelings about a wonderful man...Live and let live, Percy always used to say, and I agree!'

There'd been no confrontations at the Settlement, none that Vaughan knew of, but a rift seemed to have taken place. It was as if the town had slowly and silently split into two parts. Two opposing camps. Those who wanted to be with the Pastor of the Church of the Most Cherished Spirits, and those who did not.

Well, it was okay for some, Vaughan reasoned, if they wanted to be with the Pastor night and day. Communal barbeques and community singing and all that stuff. But why should the others feel outsiders in their own town, threatened in some way? Live and let live was not what the Pastor was doing according to Rod.

'He's getting everyone who belongs to his church to go out and round up others. You get holy Brownie points for it!'

Liam had been trying with the Nooan boys, Rod had heard, and one or two of them had actually joined the church. This had really impressed some of the undecided townspeople. If he could change that lot, he could change anybody!

Fine for the Nooan boys he'd never got to know, fine for the younger boys that had formed Liam's circle. Let them all go and live over there at the Compound and pray together or whatever. But now his grandmother was clearly thinking of moving. She was wearing the purple scarf the

Pastor had given all the women in his flock. They were dotting the streets, little unwelcome slashes of colour separating old friends. He'd said this to January who was standing at the door of their kitchen, looking out into the sandhills, still for once, on this breathless morning air.

'Well, maybe that's for the best,' she said evasively. 'It's like a club, I suppose. Belonging.'

'You wouldn't leave here, would you?' he'd asked her. The blue of the sea was fathomless, alluring, and he knew he'd be off swimming once he'd finished his chores, scuba diving if he could find Rod. But he had to have this out with her.

'You said you couldn't leave the house. You said so. Because of Grandfather, your memories of him.'

'I know,' she agreed. 'That's the main obstacle for me. Percy and I had such good times here. And it seems this house has supported me through the bad times too.'

Vaughan looked up at the ageing photograph in its fake tortoiseshell frame on the wall above the sideboard. He wondered what his grandfather would make of all of this, of January's obvious adoration of this man.

'But the Pastor said I should face up to it—the final separation before the coming together again,' his grandmother was musing aloud. 'He said we could face up to it together. With the help of brothers and sisters, not just here either, but round the world! Vaughan, think of that, there are Believers all round the world. We could surmount it. The pain of this loss, any loss, my dear.'

She turned to him her eyes lit up in that way again. 'He says if we work and pray together we can build a whole new village, a whole new town for Believers! So making a move now, even though it's hard, would prove I can be part of that.'

She looked so happy when she said this, he could almost agree. But something, something he'd not yet quite fathomed, was wrong with this cosy arrangement. Something was horribly wrong, and he could only say things he and Rod had discussed, and what his instinct on meeting the man who called himself the Pastor had told him.

'You know how much he wants you to be part of the Cherished Family too. Anyway, he's planning on starting up a school. Now we've heard that the old one's closing down for sure, that's the one you'd be going to—'

'I won't be here much longer,' Vaughan answered stubbornly.

'Vaughan, when are you going to face it—they're not coming back.'

'Who says? They told you?' The claw of fear made his voice sharp.

'No, they didn't tell me, they don't need to...'

When he could get away, he took a ragged towel and sprinted across the sand despite the heat. Towards Madshark, surf either side to choose from, and the place where Rod was likely to turn up any time. He dived underwater, counting the seconds as always, allowing his breath to come out easy, nice and slow, curving to the surface to gulp in the air when his lungs ached with longing, and then resubmerging. When he'd exhausted himself measuring some small improvement in his time, he made for the shore and lay on the sand trying not to think of the last letter from his mother.

Dear Vaughan,

You'll be surprised to get so many letters from me I know, but I've got to where I look forward to putting pen to paper. Like it's a bit of a story unfolding. I'm going to try to write a letter a day to you this week! How's that? A quiet time between the acts.

House of Blues has asked me to stay a few more weeks and then go on to their other place in Las Vegas for a while. Well, we'll see. School starts soon for you love and your dad and I think you should stay put—just another six months. And then we'll be coming home flush. Get us a nice place up north—

It was never going to happen. His grandmother was right. There'd be another gig and another six months and then another. They'd never come home and he'd have to stick with this place and the Pastor forever.

His grandmother might hang out for a few more months but she thought she was going to heaven with that creep. Eventually she would move in. He'd work on her, the slimy Pastor, and soon they'd be over there—one big happy family. He had to get away from here and bugger the Pastor's school, the charlatan Pastor, and the dive!

'So what is he promising, Gran?' he asked her at lunch. Toast and sardines again. There'd been a lack of food lately in the house and she'd seemed upset when he'd commented about it. He knew his mother and father were always slow with the money. He didn't like to ask. 'So what is he promising?' he repeated.

'You're a young cynic, you know that, Vaughan? I can hear the cynicism in your voice right now. You don't really want to know but I'll tell you anyways.' Her face brightened.

'He said the seas will be bountiful here if we pray together.'

'If the driftnets are stopped, Nan, if the driftnets go!' Vaughan found himself almost yelling.

'Yes, well maybe that too…but who told you about the driftnets?'

'Rod Chi. He said that big company up the coast had fished the place out and you'd need powerful boats to go right out to sea these days!'

'Oh Rod Chi, what would he know? Pastor said that lot's dysfunctional. He and his mum and his half-sister, Nona. All eyes, she is, for Liam nowadays, that one. She's a half-caste you know. And she can be a sulky little thing too. But the Pastor says he could probably change that! The whole family need a lot of work on them and he sees it as a particularly difficult but interesting challenge. One he'd welcome of course! He's wonderful that way…specially when that woman tries to stir up trouble against him the way she does.'

Vaughan certainly didn't want a diatribe about the Chis. 'What else does he say?'

'You should come to the prayer meetings and then you'd know,' she said but she told him anyway. 'We'd be a community again. Something you wouldn't know about. People caring for one another. Like the old days, only better. Loving and sharing and no fears of ageing and being left alone. A Divine Family. And in a few years, just a few— a very rich family. Don't you laugh. It's all possible. They've communities set up all over the world. Small ones, but gaining in popularity. Ours could be a model one.'

'And what exactly does he share with you? The Pastor?'

'So like your father, Vaughan. In so many annoying little ways. His time, that's what he shares with us! The Pastor has nothing earthly. At least, not yet.' And the way she smiled at that worried him more than what she was saying.

Yesterday, as she'd set out for yet another prayer meeting, he'd seen her drop her bankbook stuffed with notes, into her bag. 'The man has to live, Vaughan,' she'd said a little guiltily. 'It's a small thing to ask.' And then she'd added as if to legitimise it, 'And anyway, it's none of your business...'

But he thought it was his business. The food for one thing. The rip-off for another. When he could, he'd got to the bankbook and seen that her pension cheque had been halved for the past three weeks! How many more in the town, he wondered, thought they were building an Eternal City with their Pastor?

Yes, she'd have to go over there in the end. She wouldn't be able to survive, to pay the gas and the light bills. The Pastor was seeing to that!

It had been three days now since Rod had come to swim with him at Madshark. Vaughan finally decided to call at his house. The two of them walked quickly down the lane, already awash with afternoon sand, towards the empty beach, towels over their shoulders.

'Looks like Liam's planning to go over there for good!' Rod didn't need to say where.

'You mean of his own free choice?'

'Yeah, I don't get it. Didn't say a bloody thing to me! He

was alone a couple of weeks after his aunt left and now he's staying over there with the holy nerd.'

'Is your sister...is Nona going over there too?' But Rod ignored the question, his thoughts on Liam.

'We both cacked ourselves at the antics of that damned preacher, that first meeting. And now Liam doesn't want to know me.' Rod was silent a moment as if grasping at a reason. 'Look, it might be just a passing mood. See, Liam has a problem sometimes—he gets depressed. Seriously depressed.

'Once they had to put him in one of those looney bin places for a few weeks. Out of the blue, on account of something that happened to him long time ago, he can go down. Feel real low. I just leave him be then. So that's what I thought this was about.' Rod's handsome face still had a puzzled expression. 'But then next thing I hear he's spending more and more time with the Pastor. And now, today, I hear he's more or less moved over there.'

'He's got my gran going. She's well and truly hooked,' Vaughan put in.

'We're mates.' Rod didn't seem to be listening to Vaughan's worries. 'We go back a long way. But he hasn't said a damn word to me about all this.'

'It's not like he's leaving town,' Vaughan said thinking of the impossible stretch of ocean that was separating him from his parents. 'He's not that far away. Maybe you can talk some sense into him.'

'It's forever and the abyss,' Rod said gloomily, 'if he goes over there for good.'

'Well, my grandmother's thinking of going there, too!'

'Shit!' He'd heard Vaughan this time.

'Exactly!'

'That means you'd have to go over there.'

'Get lost! I'd track down my parents first. Get out of here.'

'My mum's out of a job now. And another lot of families, not Compound families, are leaving because of the school thing. Kids have to board at the next town which is a long way so they're quitting the Settlement.'

'My grandmother says the Pastor's opening his own school,' Vaughan offered.

'Mum thinks he's a real crackpot,' Rod went on. 'She's trying to find stuff on him, his past, in the States where he said he'd been before. The organisation, Cherished Spirits stuff. But so far she's found nothing. Mum's dead scared Nona'll end up over there with him.'

Vaughan had seen Nona once or twice round the town and she'd always smiled at him though they'd never spoken again. He hadn't had the courage. But he felt somehow they still shared something. A useless secret maybe, but something.

'She adopted?' he asked. 'Your sister?'

'Yeah, obviously!' Rod spoke almost angrily.

Vaughan had almost blazed back at him, 'Not to me, it's not! I've never seen any photo of your damned father, to know if he were Aboriginal or not.' But something made him hold back. Rod was already so agitated.

'She and Liam...you know they're an item now, last few months. My mum's read the riot act to her, about being too young, but it's no use. Once Nona makes up her mind there's no changing her. Even Mum knows that. She's real worried about Nona. I've told her Liam's a good bloke underneath. Now I don't know. For three years, I saw him every second day. Then he up and disappears like this...'

The sun played on the surface of the smooth sea and in the distance the shed on the little jetty gleamed invitingly. If trouble were in the air, in the calm and warmth of a perfect summer's day, it seemed the whole bay was unaware of it.

'Wanna dive?' Rod asked.

'Okay Professional and Certified Diving Instructor!' Vaughan laughed. 'Maybe the Pastor should get into this!'

'Funny you should say that. Nona says he's mad on spear fishing.'

The Pastor was soon out of their thoughts as they went gliding over the shimmering marine shapes impossible to be seen in the upper world. Both boys found that everything flowed away, worries and doubts and problems, as they shared the world below. Time out. But an hour or so later, as they were stacking their gear, neatly as Rod had demonstrated, into the rickety fisherman's shed, Rod's face was already gloomy.

'You swim with Liam or the others any more?' Vaughan knew the little group seemed to have melted away.

'Nah, there is no gang any more. You can forget doing that dive, you know that.'

Vaughan didn't like to say he felt a sense of relief. The only diving he wanted to do was the kind they were doing today. Every day if he could.

On his way home that afternoon, Vaughan went via the township and came face to face with Nona Chi. She was coming down the hill from the church with a few others who walked on, hardly acknowledging him.

'Hullo Vaughan Roberts,' Nona said, smiling at him in a way that made his heart miss a beat.

'I...we...Rod was just telling me...' he blushed, awkward, not sure of what to say.

'I've just been to band practice up there,' she indicated the church. 'You should maybe come up one afternoon. It's a great band, you know.'

'Too busy,' he smiled at her.

'Rod tells me you've taken to diving.' He felt ridiculously pleased that Rod was discussing him with her at all. 'Just as well, cause there's not much else to do round here, is there?'

'Madshark's a top beach,' he said.

'You should try Backbeach sometime.' She was walking in step with him now.

'Backbeach?'

'On past Madshark. A bit of a walk, but there's a natural rock pool there—usually calm—good for training. Best in the morning before the wind comes up,' and she was off again with a wave of her hand.

He liked that invitation far better and wondered if she knew about his training for the dive too. He went to Backbeach the very next morning. It was another stretch of empty sand, miles of it fringed with tough grass and low salty scrub, with a good surf rolling in. But down at the rockpool she'd spoken of he could see two figures. One of them was Nona's as he'd hoped, but the other was a young man. It had to be Liam. Yes, it was for sure. They were standing on a rock ledge talking, Liam's arm round Nona's shoulders. Somehow he couldn't face the two of them.

Before they had a chance to catch sight of him, Vaughan turned back.

At Madshark he threw himself into surfing with a vengeance. Beyond the breakers, in the deep green water, he began practising his long underwater stints again. He mightn't be doing any dive for Liam's sake now, but it made him feel powerful to skim through the underwater with such strong even strokes, releasing the air, 'slow as, mate, slow as...' the way Rod had taught him. And it helped wash away the image that had so needled him, of Nona and Liam together.

NINE

Rod jumped in fright when Sandy Mason emerged from a shop doorway, well before Rod was in sight of the Compound. He felt jangled anyway. Nona had gone missing and he'd found her at Liam's house, curled up asleep, her face on his friend's old shirt like a puppy trying to scent its master.

'Hey, Nona, Mum wants you.' When she sat up he saw the graze on her forehead and saw drops of blood congealed on the shirt.

'What the hell happened to you?'

'Liam asked me to wait for him here. I waited but he didn't come. So I went over there.'

'I reckon Liam'll be back here. He'd never go over there permanently. It's only a phase!' Rod was still trying to convince himself.

'Never say never, Rod.'

'So did you find him?'

'They threw rocks at me. All the little kids, twelve-year-olds. The gates are back on and there's wire all around now. Even though the gates are open those little brats wouldn't let me in this time.'

'But didn't someone stop them—adults?'

'Everyone seemed to evaporate. Worst of all I thought I saw Liam's face at the window. I'm not sure. But he didn't come out even though I screamed out his name. I went ballistic I guess. I screamed it over and over.'

'Why don't you go home? Mum's worried. I'll find Liam and tell him what happened in his precious Compound. Those kids should be—'

'Funny isn't it, when the Pastor says he's on about loving fellowship? I don't know what to make of the place.'

Rod stared at his sister. 'Nona, don't even think of it!' he warned. 'You couldn't hack it in the Compound. You of all people, you like to be free. There're a heap of rules and they're writing more and more for those stupid sods over there. How to tie your shoelaces, I bet!'

She managed to laugh at this.

'I'm serious, Nona. You couldn't hack it!' he repeated.

'I know I want to be with Liam. He needs someone.'

He knew it would be impossible to fight with her now so he nodded, humouring her. 'Look, let me go talk to him first. Okay? Those little turds won't dare throw rocks at me!'

They went out into the night together and he watched her a moment to make sure she was heading back to the deserted side of the village. It was as if it were a town rent asunder by this man and, he thought grimly, there were only a few more seams to rip apart to complete its destruction. What was worse, it seemed even Nona was weakening.

'Tell him to come for me tonight. Tell him I need to talk to him,' Nona insisted.

Rod put his head down, for the wind was freshening, a sandstorm brewing, and made his way briskly though the deserted streets.

That was when someone stepped out of the shadows and grabbed him. A hand across his mouth, TV cop show style. When he wrenched himself away he was relieved to see it was Sandy.

'What's that all about?' he began.

'Speak quiet or he'll hear.'

'Who?' But Rod knew.

'My mum loves being over there with the Pastor more and more every day.' Sandy was breathing hard, his blood-shot eyes bulging with fear. 'But I'm not bloody well staying. I'm working out a way to get out of there.' He motioned Rod into the doorway of a broken-down shop where they sheltered from the wind.

'He's a psycho, that Pastor, but my mum—all of them—think he's a bloody god! He biffs you as soon as looks at you. Troublemakers he calls us. Not Liam. No way! He seems to hate me even though he says over and over he—' here the boy paused, looked down.

'What? What does he say?'

'He takes me aside and—ugh! He says he...he *loves* me!'

Rod laughed. 'Well, he's got a strange bloody way of showing it. Locking you up like he does and—' Sandy's eyes were downcast but Rod could see one of them was swollen purple, bruised. 'And you walked into a door I suppose?'

'Man of God did this and he locked me up in the laundry again. But I got out this time.' Sandy clenched his fist and Rod could see his knuckles were scraped and bloody.

'I thought I'd come to your place and tell you things, I reckon you and your mum should know…things I couldn't say to you the other day.' He looked around anxiously. 'But halfway to your place, I thought it was a stupid idea. Might be seen. So I hid here and then I saw you and your sister…'

'The whole place has gone mad.' Rod sat down in the windy doorway beside Sandy. The younger boy spoke rapidly as if time were running out for him.

'He can change just like that. One minute all charm and telling you you're a chosen bugger and lucky to be there, and the next—' he pointed to his eye. 'He tells them and he tells me it's purifying. That's his word—purifying. If a bashing's purifying, I'm an angel, must be. Huh! Putrefying, more like.' Rod had never heard Sandy so vociferous, watched the muscles working in his cheeks as he spoke as if he were holding back screams or tears.

'And you know what's worse? You know what I hate? I hate it when it's all calm and charm with him! Hate that bit. Lying round on mats listening to tinkly music and chanting his rubbish. And then he talks. My God does he talk! He says the exact opposite to Father James about everything. Sex, love, marriage, the lot. Lots about brotherly and sisterly love. Long as you've got condoms, then you should let it all happen! It's spooky the way he talks about all that.'

'What d'you mean?'

'Same time he says this, he says once you've satisfied your "youthful" lust by having lots of it, then you can be purified. And if guys want to stay purified—become a priest, and some of us will—then, well, it's a sacrifice for life. A sacrifice we should be thinking about if we want to enter the realms of the godly.'

'You should all be priests or what?' Rod asked.

'Seems to me he's saying lots of things I don't understand.'

'What else?'

'Look we're s'posed to go and talk about our sex problems to him—after our Life Strategy classes—but I haven't had that pleasure. I can't look him in the eyes somehow and he knows it.'

'You have classes?'

'Yeah, it's run a bit like an army camp over there now. He's organised them that way. Everything on clockwork. Meals, classes, prayers, lovemaking. But it's mad. Nobody seems to twig but me that he's mad. And I reckon he's a sleaze!'

'Why haven't you left, then?'

'I'm that bloody scared of him, mate, I can tell you!'

Rod looked at Sandy. His face was pale, boyish and defenceless. He would liked to have taken his hand.

'Pastor told me he has divine powers. Says he knows I'm possessed by evil spirits. Says he'll know wherever I go. And he'll come and find me and if he doesn't, the brotherhood will eventually. They'll bring me back. And no one on earth can stop what he'll do to me then.'

'You believe that crap?' Rod was furious. 'How would he know where you went?'

'Cherished Voices speak to him every day.'

'Sort of a divine news report, mate?'

'Don't laugh. He's mad. Dangerous mad. And I'm bloody

scared of him. You should be too. And most of all poor
bloody Vaughan Roberts.'

'What about Vaughan?' Rod's skin was prickling. He tried
to keep the urgency out of his voice but it was apparent.

'What about Vaughan?'

'He's furious he won't come over with his gran. Talks
about him, says boys like him with a wild spirit will come
to no good.'

'So what?'

'He gets his way, that man. And he wants everyone—but
everyone—over there. And maybe Vaughan Roberts a bit
more than the others!'

'Too bad! Vaughan's not going.'

'I dunno.' Sandy was uneasy.

'The Pastor can't hear you. And he sure as hell can't see
you,' Rod tried to reassure Sandy, for every so often the
boy's head jerked around the shop doorway as if he was
expecting the Pastor to be there, standing over them. 'He
can't! Not in this sandstorm. So just relax. He can't hear a
word. And he can whistle in the wind for Vaughan Roberts,
too.'

'When we do the praying thing, everyone goes funny.'
Sandy was staring straight ahead as he spoke.

'Liam?'

'Yeah, Liam, Tom, Shane, Dyson—all of 'em.'

'You?'

'No, I'm right out of it. I pretend 'cause he likes that and
I can see his eye on me. Listen, mate, I want to go wherever it is they go with him. I really do. But it's still the seedy
ballroom of the old pub to me and no matter how hard I
try, I know I'm right there. He says we can become godly.

But the more he says it I know I'm all too flesh and blood. That I still hurt—hell, yes I know that! And I don't want to be a priest. I just want to go back—' Sandy's voice was breaking and Rod put a kindly hand on his arm. '—and be, you know, ordinary again.'

'What about Liam?'

'Liam.' Sandy chewed nervously for a moment on his injured knuckle. 'God man! He sways around and he sweats like mad. Wish I could but I don't. And one night he fainted! Passed out, pissed himself too. The Pastor fusses over Liam a treat, it's sickening. After the praying and God stuff, it goes on and on. I thought old Father James was boring but this—'

'What happens after?'

'He talks to us like we're mates. The others seem to want to talk to him and I go along with it, mate. I go along, but lots of it's looney tune.'

'What sort of thing?' Rod had never felt so old, as if he were a police officer questioning a suspect. Not a Settlement police officer though, for many of them had been the first to go over to the Compound with their families.

'Lots about how we can change the Settlement and make it a Perfect Place. Make the fish bite for the fishermen, that sort of crap. But most of all about being a family. About being prepared to suffer and to give for the common good. Give up your own will for the will of the Cherished Ones. Funny thing is, sometimes when he says it over and over, and I'm busting for a leak and not allowed to go, or I'm faint with hunger because you can only eat when he says you can—sometimes, I find myself sort of believing what he says. He talks about being at peace and it sounds, well, it sounds the cool thing to be.'

'And then?'

'When I get away again, I remember the last beating he gave me and how his eyes look when he says there's a devil in me and he's going to beat it out of me! I lift up my shirt and I look at the bruises and they don't feel too bloody good even now.

'God, I couldn't stand up for a few days, it was that bad when he came at me. He kind of went real crazy, I reckon. That's what my mum said. She cried when she saw me but then she said—after a long talk with him, mind you—that it was "best" for me in the long run. And that now we could become good mates. It was up to me! That's what my mum says,' and he gave a hollow laugh, 'it's up to me.

'I think about how he beats up the little kids sometimes. And all the mums—gone mad seems to me—think it's somehow all right. Sometimes they stop him when they can't bear the cries. But not often. And he enjoys it, that's the worst of it. That's what I remember when I feel I'm weakening, and that stops me going looney tune as well.'

'Makes it tough for you though?' Rod asked sympathetically, amazed that Sandy Mason of all people...

'But Liam and the others. You wouldn't believe how they've changed in a couple of days. I don't dare say a word against the Pastor now. I know the Pastor is training Liam to be a High Priest on the religious side, which he says is the ultimate honour. And then trying to get him in as a friend on the other.'

'A follower, not a friend,' Rod felt indignant.

'Whatever. But Dyson, shit mate, he just follows Liam

anyways. They all do and I'm trapped there and that's the problem.' Then he leaned forward like a conspirator. 'Do you know what I think? He wants Liam because if he gets Liam he gets all of us. But it's more than that. He gets the Nooan boys too. I can hear him working on Liam about them all the time.'

Rod's mind was racing. Of course that was part of his plan. Every able bodied young man in the town over there inside the Compound. Perfect company and on his side— good workers too! And Liam the key to it.

'And you want to know what he says about you? The Pastor?'

Why did Rod experience such a creeping feeling at his neck? Not the sand rasping against his collar, but prickles of real fear. 'What's that?' and his own voice sounded croaky.

'Look, I know it's all shit, but the way he says it!'

'What? The way he says what?' He felt a surge of anger, felt like shaking the boy who'd subsided into silence for the moment.

'Tell me, Sandy.'

'He told us he's seen a dark shadow round you and your mum,' Sandy burst out.

'Really? A dark shadow, hey? Do you see it? Does anyone else?' Rod demanded angrily.

'No, course I don't. But he says that's what made your dad, you know…' Sandy frowned, 'hang himself like that.' Sandy's voice had dropped in deference to the subject. But Rod felt a new fury. The Pastor had said that and set up cogwheels of doubt, even in the mind of the poor fearful boy hiding out here in his misery.

'That's crap, Sandy, and you know it. My dad was a manic depressive all of his life and—'

'No need to tell me, mate. I'm just repeating what he's saying about you lot. About all the ones who don't come over.'

'Yeah, well quite a few have left town. It's kinda split the town, hasn't it? Those left here have got to go his way or go away!'

'But you haven't and that's what he says to everyone.' Sandy stood up preparing to go back out into the wind storm.

'You know what I think and that's why I'm shit scared— think something bad is going to happen. Real bad. And I know this much. I don't want to be alone on the other side like you and your mum when it does happen. So I've got to go along with it. I've got to try—hell, I'm trying—or get out of there.'

Sandy stopped speaking for a moment. He looked like a little kid who needed a big brother to comfort him but Rod, his mind racing, didn't know how.

'You and Liam, you guys were kind of gods to me,' Sandy was saying now. 'Not in that way—the religious way—but you were guys I wanted to be like. And now he's changed Liam, made him loopy and he's saying things about you, and I don't know...'

'Sandy listen to me. He's a brainwasher, the old Pastor, from way back. You're the only one in the whole Compound who's cottoned on to that. You're the one strong and brave. Not Liam and not me. Sandy it's *you*. And you've gotta stay that way, okay?'

'I'm a coward and you know it. Couldn't even do the dive.'

'You're here, right now, aren't you?'

Sandy looked around fearfully. He wiped his hand across his nose.

'But I shouldn't be. He damn near broke my arm and he said next time—'

Rod stood beside him and put his arm round the shaking shoulders. 'You are doing real, real good. You know that. And I'm going to work it so you come with us, get out of this place. Okay? When we go.'

'You mean that?' The boy stood up straight for the first time.

'Sure I mean it.'

'I don't wanna go back there. There's filthy talk with Liam and with Dyson. About the Devil's Gullet.'

Another creeping wave of fear.

'I gotta go. Get back inside that dumphole before he knows I'm outside of it.'

'You tell me first about the Devil's Gullet.'

The boy paused. 'Not sure yet, but we go down there every day to the rocks.'

'What for?'

'He's teaching us spear fishing and other things, but you gotta do it his way. In formation. Certain actions. He even manages to make that bloody boring. Standing for hours in the sun in a line. I don't know what he's up to.'

'You don't have to go back there you know. You could come home with me right now.'

The boy was making quick anxious glances out into the road again and suddenly darted off but not before he called over his shoulder, 'I'll come back *here* tomorrow, okay. Tell you more then.'

Rod knew it was the best he could get from Sandy right now. He watched the boy speeding along the street through the spittle of rain, his heavy heels sending up anxious flurries of sand. He knew his own heart was beating as fearfully as Sandy's. But poor bloody Sandy had to face the dumphole for several hours more, and then the Pastor.

TEN

Sometimes it could be almost pleasant at night in the old house after dinner. Just the two of them in the lounge room, the only room with all its windows intact. Vaughan's grandmother in a softer mood, the wine making her smile a little, the music Vaughan had unearthed and put on the old player, making her smile quite a lot.

He liked using the antique record player, liked the way the great big black discs dropped onto the turntable and the arm moved over onto the surface, the loud anticipatory crackle of needle on vinyl before the strains of *Showboat* or *Gigi* or *My Fair Lady* or some other American musical filled the air. Some of the songs he knew word perfect, his father had sung them so often. Sometimes his grandmother would tell stories about his grandfather or, if he were really lucky, tales of his dad. But tonight Vaughan could see his grandmother was quiet, thoughtful.

'Why were you called January, Nan?' he asked her.

'My name was going to be April if I'd been on time, even though I'd have been born in December. But my parents were that pleased to have their first child on the first day of a new year—1919, end of the Great War—they called me January. Later my dad told me Janus the Roman god was always the first to receive a portion of the sacrifice. Always the first. I told the Pastor that bit and he was that interested.

'And why was Dad called Jasper?' he asked, steering her away from the Pastor, the Compound and the Church of the Most Cherished Spirits.

'It's a family name. Your grandfather did a stint at Lightning Ridge, the opal mine. He didn't find any opals but he found jasper. He was that pleased since it was his name too. Look, I've still got a piece,' and she hurried away to get a fine gold necklace, from which hung a colourful piece of quartz, to show him.

'Why don't you wear it?' he asked, hating the clumsy coral piece she'd taken to wearing. She fingered the coral a little nervously he thought.

'Vaughan, I want to talk to you seriously. And tonight might be the night!'

'Not about the Pastor, Nan.'

'I'm praying for your mum and dad, you know.'

'Why?' he asked surprised.

'They won't be coming back here and they need any help they can get where they are.

There was that familiar feeling of panic at her words.

'And the Pastor has been kind enough—'

'I'm not going over there. I've told you that.'

'—kind enough to offer to take full responsibility for you should anything happen to me.'

'I don't need his kindness and I'll take responsibility for myself.'

'Oh Vaughan, Vaughan. I'm too old to fight these battles. What have you got against the man anyway? His message is only ever about good.' She was being strangely patient with him tonight and he didn't like it. Better the sharp tongue than honeyed words.

She sat there looking at him with a kind of reasonable, slightly hurt expression and for the moment he floundered. What did he have against the Pastor? The message was one of hope and prosperity for all, true enough. So what was it about this person that repulsed him in every way? And then he thought of the man's actions, the truth of the matter, of Sandy, and what Rod had told him about Sandy and the Pastor.

'He's a bully,' the words were out before he could choose more carefully. 'And a slime and that's got to mean he's bloody dishonest!'

'Watch your language, young man,' she began. 'I'm telling you all of this for your own good. And it upsets me you won't listen. He feels you need to be taken in hand, not left to run wild the way you do. And to tell you the truth I agree. I don't want a repetition of Jasper Roberts on my hands. And some of the young people over there have benefited so much from a father figure.'

'He locked Sandy up. Beat him up badly and locked him in a laundry for hours! Is that a benefit? He beats little kids!' Vaughan was incredulous.

She smiled at this, 'Sometimes you have to be cruel to be kind, you know.'

'I know what's kind and what's uncalled-for cruelty. And you should too!'

He had the strangest sensation his grandmother was listening but not hearing in the way he wanted. That she was storing every word he said and over tea with the Pastor tomorrow or next week would faithfully report all of it.

'It's very likely I'll join the family over there, Vaughan. At my age, well, there are good reasons to be part of a loving community you know. And for you there's an education and training, more of a future.'

'I'd rather get a job on a garbage truck than go live with that—'

'That's enough of that talk, Vaughan. Enough!'

'And Mum and Dad haven't pissed off either. They're not dead and gone to heaven if that's what you're thinking. They're coming back for me.'

The patronising smile she gave him terrified Vaughan. She didn't speak. How come the Pastor had her confidence—no, more than that—her love? And Rod's friend, Liam's for that matter!

Vaughan was defeated and left her there, teacup in hand, the strains of 'Old Man River' following him to his bedroom. He sat on the bed. Thoughts of his parents unnerved him. Where the hell were they?

'*Tired...living...scared...dying,*' the words rang out at him. He got up and closed the door but the music persisted until quite late.

That night Vaughan's sleep was fitful. Faces, underwater faces, haunted him again, all of them different, some of them looking in a frightening way like Liam, or like the dreaded Pastor. And then the one he'd seen before, the featureless, horrifying face with its wide drowned mouth. No, not that! Vaughan had the sensation of submerging, woke afraid and breathless. He rose and went outside, glad of the cold wind from the sea and the angry crash of a stormy sea. He wouldn't be small and afraid. Somehow he had to work out a way to keep his grandmother clinging on here until he located his parents. He would not go over there where he knew Sandy's fate awaited him. He would not.

ELEVEN

No one tried to stop Rod's entry to the Compound but Liam was simply not to be found. Rhonda was tense when Rod reached home again.

'I can't find Nona. She came home, helped me with some sorting out then said she was tired and she was going to watch television. But she's gone again!'

'Back to Liam, maybe at his place,' Rod said.

'Look, I know he's your friend, was your friend until...' his mother faltered but then went on. 'But Nona seems...well...I'm worried sick, despite what she says, that she'll end up in that cult. Because of what she feels for Liam!'

'I'll go look for her if you want.'

'No!' His mother's voice was sharp. 'I mean, don't go just now. I want to talk to you.'

'What is it?'

Rhonda Chi, obviously not herself, began moving rest-
lessly round the hot room, plucking at things, straightening
a cushion needlessly. She stopped suddenly and looked up
at him as if resolving something for herself.

'We're leaving here,' she told him.

'I know that, Mum. And I'm not worried. Nona'll get
used to the idea too. The place's gone to the dogs now.
Talk about a split—it's a landslide, I reckon! To the Pastor,
wholesale. You said you needed some time to get everything arranged?'

'No, I'm not waiting. I want to go and I want to go now.'

'Right now? Why?' Again that strange feeling, his heart
missing a beat. Had somebody repeated the insane stuff
Sandy had told him? Or had she witnessed yet another
family quietly moving out of town, not saying much just
going?

'Wait, I want to show you something.'

Rod felt trepidation as his mother left the room. She
looked frightened and that meant things *had* got back to
her. The Pastor's theory. But why should it frighten him? It
did and now he felt fury rising at the way this was affecting
his mother.

She'd already been through so much. Sometimes she
was hard to get on with, she could be so forceful. But he
understood and so did Nona that the death of their dad
would have been unbearable if it hadn't been for her. Her
compassion and then her toughness, her determination to
get on with things though it had seemed life was shattered.
She'd carried his dad, he knew that, she'd carried him for
years. Time and again through his manic phases she'd
somehow managed with such fortitude. How dare this

lousy, two-bit town take her down like this! How dare this crummy Pastor and his motley flock mention his mother and *evil* in the same breath. They *would* get out as soon as they could and to hell with Liam.

Strange, it had been Rhonda Chi who had been pleased to stop a while here at the Settlement with her new job. When they might have left in the second year, she said she was relieved to see Nona settled into school at last, and doing so well. They'd been told very early that Nona was highly gifted but she'd never liked school until this one. Whereas Rod hadn't liked the feel of the place from the first moment and he'd said so.

'The Settlement might be a place for us to stay *settled* a while, Rod,' she'd said with a wry smile when she'd agreed to renew her contract. 'Nona's getting on so well at school. You'll be through next year and then we can think again.' Since the death of his dad she'd spoken to him about family matters of importance. So he'd agreed, despite his misgivings. By then he'd met Liam and the place hadn't seemed so bad.

Whatever had happened in the last few hours to change her like this must be to do with what Sandy had relayed to him, Rod guessed. Poor bloody Sandy. They should try to take him out of here, too. But Vaughan was the one who needed an escape route more urgently. There were machinations about Vaughan for sure, and his stupid grandmother must be going along with it. Escape route? This was crazy thinking. They weren't trapped. They were free to go like the other families who'd moved out over the last few days. Free.

Rhonda came back clutching a letter and he could see blotches of colour on her neck, a sure sign she was upset.

'I have to show you what kind of thinking's going on round here because it's affecting all of us.'

'Who's it from? That creep?'

She shook her head. 'Anonymous but it reeks of Compound thinking.'

You and your superior kids should come behind the wire, try to beg entrance from the Master. He's told us that you, Rhonda Chi, are the cause of your husband's suicide. Your evil thoughts. He sees an aura of evil round you every time you walk on the street. And there's one growing round your kids as well. They should not be left in your hands. They need guidance.

They need the Pastor's firm hand of discipline and the prayers of a community at one, as you need his strength and guidance. Your son is being corrupted by his friendship with the newcomer, which is why he is resisting. Your daughter is unruly, reflecting some of your outspoken views but he feels she can be changed through her friendships here.

You should talk to your children firmly. Do it soon because there could be dire consequences for anyone here who continues to resist goodness. The Ascendant Cherished Spirits will be angry with people like you who are openly hostile and they might punish you. Or worse still, your kids. You need the purification and the supplication the Master offers.

This is friendly advice, for the moment. Put on the purple scarf and come begging or there could be another tragedy in your family. And it will be your own fault.

'It's a bloody threat of a letter! Take it to the police,' Rod tried to keep his voice calm but his hand shook as he dropped the letter on the table. It felt a dirty and dishonourable thing to touch. 'I've already heard the same kind of thing!'

At this her face looked grey and much older. 'I phoned Sergeant Wilson straight away. Mrs Wilson was there. She sounded strange. She said her husband had left his post as senior police officer here yesterday. Resigned. And the replacement would be coming next few days. And you know why? Rod, you know why?'

'The Compound?'

'He and Mrs Wilson and the kids,' she nodded solemn faced. 'And Rod, when I tried to phone the police at Cat Harbour to report this—' He saw her eyes dark with fear.

'What Mum? What did they say?'

'The phone is not making long distance connections due to 'faults'. It can't be a coincidence.'

'Bloody hell,' Rod sank down in the chair.

'Yet when I consider things logically, there's no reason to think anyone would want to detain us here. What's the point when they know my feelings about the Pastor? Unless it's a crazy kind of point of honour for him. A saving face thing. Or maybe he knows I've been trying to get information about him, maybe he thinks I have it to hand. I don't know. Anyway, something tells me we should get out as soon we can!'

'In a few days you mean?'

She shook her head.

'Today?' he was surprised at her sense of urgency but he had to agree. 'How much petrol in the car?'

'That's the trouble. Just about empty. We have to get some from Clemens' Garage when they open tomorrow. At least he's still running the place, though for how long? I'll go there just as normal. We've got to think things through carefully. Not panic about it. Pack what we need in here so no one sees. No one knows. It's best that way.'

'There *is* no one much to see. I mean just about everyone's gone over to him. A few cats and stray dogs and us left, eh?' He laughed, wanting to relax the tension in the room but his mother frowned.

'I don't want to go on about it, but I feel like someone's watching us, even now.' And she jumped up nervously to pull the curtains closed. 'I've started packing some things already—clothes mainly, and our books and photos. But we won't attempt to leave until after dark tomorrow. With a tankful of petrol.'

'I'll go find Nona, now.'

'Don't alarm her. I'll tell her when we're on our way.'

'She won't leave Liam easily. We'll have to think of some excuse to get out of here.'

'Be careful, Rod. After a letter like that I don't really know what to think. No, it's the opposite, isn't it?' She looked at him searchingly, 'I know exactly what to think!'

'Vaughan Roberts should come with us. I think they've got it in for him too. His grandma's thick as thieves with the Pastor.'

'No, I can't endanger you kids by including anyone else. He has his grandmother. They're not behind the wire of the Compound yet. And she doesn't seem to have an aura of evil like we do!'

TWELVE

Vaughan made his way home. He'd swum by himself all afternoon. Rod was nowhere to be found. With no urgency for the dive any more, Rod seemed less interested in being a companion swimmer or diver.

As usual, Vaughan's thoughts turned to his parents. He had determined he would not write another letter but speak to them direct. Live! Someone must know where they were. He vaguely knew they had an agent in Sydney. He'd make it his business this afternoon to track that agent down. Track *them* down then. His grandmother could help. She'd be glad to see the last of him now she was so lovey-dovey with the Pastor!

He wasn't going to stay here and his parents should know that. No, he'd not say that and be ignored as usual. He'd ask them calmly, but firmly to send the money for the air ticket to join them. Be direct about it. But his stomach felt queasy at the thought. Why, why had he always found it so hard to say to them exactly what he was feeling? Even in his letters, the ones he'd sent to the hotel his mother had mentioned, he'd always chicken out in the end. He'd still not been able to reveal his fears openly, make demands on them.

He'd told them of January's obsession with the Pastor, the rift in the town and just how he saw it. But there'd been no reply to that letter or any of the others. Big fat silence. Maybe they'd never got any of those carefully written missives? But then again maybe they had. He'd have to talk to them. It was the only way.

He walked down the track to the back door. The house seemed in some way different when he walked in. 'Nan, you there?' he called, trying to keep the urgency out of his voice. There was the same gritty feel underfoot when he kicked off his sandals. The same heat in the kitchen where things irritated him—the mildly flapping fly strips she'd instituted where the dead bodies of flies, so many unpleasant black currants, were suspended above the table; the constantly dripping tap she'd railed at him about because he didn't know how it could be mended. 'Your father didn't teach you anything useful round the house,' she'd complained and for once he'd had to agree.

He looked around. What was changed here? The tables and chairs hadn't moved, had they? The clock still tocked against the background of the constant wash of surf, out there over the hills. What was different then?

'Nan!' When he called out her name for the second time it was in a bit of a panic as if, as if he were going to find her...He ran through the house. He rarely entered her room, but he threw open the door. The bed was neat, the furniture innocent. But where the wedding picture of January and Percy had been resplendent above her bed, he saw there was just an outline. A light square against the dark and fly-spotted colour of the ancient, painted timber. Her dressing table was empty. And when he opened the wardrobe her clothes were gone.

'Shit!' he exploded feeling absolutely betrayed.

Worse was to come on his panicky exploration of the house. In his room he could see at a glance that most of his possessions were gone too. The bastard! He'd come here and talked her into it knowing he, Vaughan, was out. On his bed he found a note written in her spidery writing.

Dear Vaughan,

The Pastor is here with me now. I feel so strong and so sure about this, filled with love and hope as I know you will be when you come to join us and find out all the joy of being a Cherished One at last.

Your grandmother
January Roberts now to be known as
Most Cherished Springtime

With trembling hands he wrenched open the bottom drawer. The letters—his mother's, his father's—even the letter he was writing at the moment was gone too. He cast about him and saw another message attached to the mirror. This one was written in a firm, unfamiliar hand. Had to be the Pastor's handwriting.

Vaughan

Your grandmother, Most Cherished Springtime, was afraid to leave and come to the Cherished Ones whilst you were in the house. She sensed your hostility and disapproval. I have placated her and we have prayed together for your guidance.

We know that you will come of your own free will at the appointed hour. I thought it sensible to give you a night to your- self to think about it. I will come to the top of the hill at 7pm. Wave the cloth at the window, and I'll come down to fetch you. If you need another night to think about it, I understand.

I have sought the advice of the Most Cherished Ones and they advise that you will be with us within 24 hours.

We look forward to your arrival.

The Pastor of the Church of the Most Cherished Spirits

Go over to the bloody Compound. Not at 7 pm or 7 am! he thought indignantly, blood rushing to his head. As if he'd go willingly and join that lot. No! He wouldn't be waving any cloth at any window and specially not the purple scarf that had been left on the sill for him. He'd made that decision easily. But he was feeling scared, really scared.

Now as he roved through the lounge room, he noticed the absence of clutter. Another picture of Percy gone from above the sideboard. What else had she taken? Food? Why think of that now? But hungry as he was after his swimming exertions, he wondered if she'd cleared the kitchen cup- boards too. Just about. Three cans of beans and one of spaghetti. Well that was something. And bread left though the toaster was gone. What should he do? Try to phone his parents as he'd planned? It was really horribly urgent now. If only he knew where to find them. Phone Rod? His hand actually trembled as he listened to the unanswered repeating call at the Chi's house. Surely someone was there. He'd wait until dark and go over. He'd calm down and eat something right now. And then he'd think this through, slowly and carefully.

Vaughan cooked the can of spaghetti on a low gas. He knew he should probably only eat half of it to conserve the food stores. There'd been nobody in the shops as he'd come through the town. But he wolfed the whole lot down with the last slices of stale bread. He wouldn't stay here long.

As darkness began to fall he told himself he wasn't scared here alone. He'd been left in this house plenty of nights with the sand spitting at the windows and the wind moaning. But the weight of the heat of the day seemed to have been replaced with the heaviness of waiting and the cry of the wind that had risen so sharply.

Through the salt-smeared window he noticed that no lights lit up the houses across the way and down the hill. The families had all gone over. Must have. Why today? The Pastor had come collecting maybe.

They were all at the Compound. Even his grandmother. Maybe the whole of the town was at the Compound. Maybe he was the only one in the entire Settlement sitting in a house by himself waiting, waiting. He'd been abandoned, hadn't he? he thought ruefully. What was wrong with Vaughan Jasper Roberts the Third? First his parents had left him, and now his grandmother had dumped him too!

He looked around the cheerless kitchen. Listening to the wind revving up in the sandhills, he knew he was actually missing his grandmother, not her complaining tones, but her link to those he loved most in the world. It wasn't all bad here as she wasn't all bad either, he knew that. And in some way, with her stories of the past, she'd made him feel closer to his dad just when he was about to give up on both his parents. It was obvious now, despite her protestations, that she loved his dad in a funny kind of way, and it seemed like January had loved him too. She had felt like his family, telling those funny stories to an eager audience of one.

But Vaughan knew very well that in leaving the old house his grandmother had made the decision to leave her former life behind. Most Cherished Springtime! My God, what was all this? His father and mother simply wouldn't believe it. Leaving her former self behind and, if needs be, leaving her grandson, Vaughan Jasper Roberts the Third. Alone!

As if on cue, the wind screaming away outside bit deeper and tore at the window, snatching a plastic pane. There was a mad flurry across the table and he grabbed at a discarded prayer pamphlet that had puffed up about to take off across the room. It was like a crazy thing eager to flap in his face but he subdued it, crushing it madly in his hands and tossing it, a useless ball, angrily against the cupboard. It felt like the Pastor was reaching right inside the house.

Ridiculous, he thought, as he tacked new plastic to that fractious space not caring that it was his grandmother's gaudy orange. The Pastor had wanted her and her friends and he'd got them in the end. Working away deliberately over weeks and months, slowly and patiently. One by one they'd gone. First the eager then the doubtful. Collected, the lot of them, as he'd be collected too, if he sat round here. Vaughan knew the Pastor would be in no mind to be patient with a boy like him. He thought of the man's letter and went straight back to his grandmother's room and tore the page into tiny pieces. He felt better after he'd done it. But now what?

THIRTEEN

Nona had seen Liam in one of his depressions, but she'd never seen him acting this way. 'I've sinned again,' he was moaning over and over, 'and on the eve of my redemption. I can't believe it! I just can't believe it!'

Moments before they'd been in each others' arms and he'd been whispering love-talk to her. Now this anguished voice was like a knife cutting any bonds of tenderness. He turned to the wall, beginning to shake as if with some terrible cold despite the warmth of the evening.

She hadn't liked his insistence on coming to his room in the Centre—the old hotel in the Compound as she still called it; hadn't liked being so close to where the Pastor held his classes and held counsel with the stream of people constantly seeking his advice and his blessing.

Liam had told her that they should not go back to the house. He'd said the boys who'd thrown stones at her those weeks ago had been castigated and that it would never happen again now that nearly everyone in the town was here. No need for hostility, which the Pastor explained was natural enough towards 'outsiders'. He'd added that the Pastor was pleased with the fact she'd been coming to some of the classes, but of course he'd like her to come to more. She was to feel this was her place now too, her home.

What had puzzled Nona was Liam's physical avoidance of her. When they'd come into the room and closed the door and she'd tried to kiss him, he told her they should sit apart, Nona opposite him on the old cane chair. This had put a distance between them in every way. She could see he was agitated again, the way he had been lately with things he felt duty bound to say to her. So she didn't press the point, merely listened as he seemed to want her to do.

Liam gave his usual glowing report of what was happening in the Compound and asked her why anyone would want to stay outside of it. He told her that as far as he was concerned the town had gone, had been 'swept away' now.

'Well, our house sure hasn't. Not since last time I checked,' she'd told him, heedless of the strange look he gave her.

He told her how much he wanted her to join him here, not just for an afternoon or an evening but forever! She was taken aback at this outpouring. He still hadn't attempted to kiss her but when he'd come to her and taken her hand with this entreaty she'd not held back. She'd jumped up and embraced him eagerly. There seemed such a hunger in him that at first his responding hug was almost too strong. They'd sunk down on Liam's bed, shedding their clothes and made love, not in the same way as before. Yes, they had been passionate before, but now there seemed an added dimension, a ferocity and a sense of urgency with Liam. He'd cradled her afterwards, wept. He'd spoken of his love as she had of hers. And then suddenly he'd turned away.

'Liam, what is it? What's happening?' She tried to touch him but the hard corrugations of his spine as he curled up in a foetal position seemed a defence wall against her.

'Sin, sin, sin!' he moaned and then she understood. She sat up furious that once again the Pastor had reached into their lives, right into their love-making. The trembling passed and now he became more coherent.

'I told you not to come too close tonight of all nights and you wouldn't listen, would you?'

She couldn't believe the change in him. Wanted to block her ears as he went on.

'Now I'll have to go and confess my weakness and my sin to him. He'll be so upset, not for himself but for me. So sad for me!' He turned back towards her but his eyes stared past her.

'Listen, Liam, you don't have to tell him anything you don't want to!' Nona said with feeling. 'Liam, look at me for God's sake!' He seemed in genuine torment but she was cruel with desperation. 'I don't know you when you're like this. You're turning into a wimp and a coward and all those things you've always despised. You're turning into a weakling! That's what he's doing for you, this man you like to call the Master!'

Liam uncurled his fine long form and stopped his mutterings. Nona was glad to see the look of disbelief on his face. 'You've got it all wrong, all wrong! You shouldn't speak that way about things you don't understand. You can't have listened. Not to a word of it! Not to him!'

She was winding the sheet around her, determined. 'Oh yes, I've listened. Twice a day and sometimes three times to your Pastor's brainwashing. That's what it is you know!' His eyes blazed with anger but she forged on.

'You've never asked for an opinion from me. Not once. But now I think it's time I gave it.'

'Be careful Nona!'

'I don't agree with his ideas—all of his Life Strategies meetings or whatever fancy name he calls them. It's group hysteria, that's what my mum says and that's what I think too. I think he's a sham, your Pastor!'

'You what?' Liam was up now and pulling on his jeans, fascinated with her in a way he hadn't been for months.

'I went along with his tedious lectures. That man's self-interest is plain as day. But you all seem…I don't know…under his spell.'

Liam had gone white at this and she saw his knuckles clench.

'So why did you…?'

'I went along with all of it for you of course! To be there when you saw through it. When you started to come back…'

'Come back? Nona, are you mad? Your mother must be telling you lies about him. She doesn't even know him. And come back to what? He's made my whole life *open up*. All these people—why do you think they want to be with him? They're happy, plain and simple—happy. And I'm happy in a way I never thought possible. And you know what he says, in our private talks?'

Yes, she'd love to know because the Pastor was forever taking Liam away somewhere for their 'private prayers', as he called them.

'He says I can be completely at peace with myself. And I believe that!'

Now that she'd shown her hand to Liam, Nona found she couldn't stop. Things she'd been wanting to say for weeks and months seemed to come out without restraint.

'What's a boy of 18 want with peace—or his kind of peace? Sounds like death to me. Snap out of it, Liam, or he'll drag you down, I know it!'

'I knew you probably couldn't ever be one of us but I let you come along, Nona. You said you wanted to, and he thought with my help you could change. He was right about one thing.' There was a long pause. 'If you didn't change, then I was allowing evil into my life.'

'You think I'm evil? *Evil*? Liam, look at me for pity's sake.'

'Sex is a danger and has potential for evil in me. He told me that. It's an obstacle for me, and a serious one if I'm to enter his priesthood. And I've got to deal with it now! Or I'll never reach the state of enlightenment he has!'

'Who wants it?' she was about to retort but she saw his eyes blaze with fervour, the way they had when the Pastor worked up the congregation of young people, praying chanting and crying and being urged 'to let go, just let go,' in ways she found plain frightening.

Life Strategies classes were a disaster for Nona. Kids she'd known for years falling on the floor and writhing and moaning and jabbering like strangers...but she'd gone along with the classes and the prayer meetings to be with Liam.

When the others wept and prayed, Liam included, she'd sunk down onto the floor and closed her eyes, hoping the madness would pass swiftly. And when it did and there was silence in the room at last, she'd open her eyes again, relieved. She had realised, though, from his briefest glance in her direction, that the Pastor knew she was not one of them. She had wanted to take Liam's hand but dared not for beads of sweat would always be standing out on his brow after these sessions, and his face would be convulsed for minutes on end until the Pastor's chanting tones eased something out of him. Only when his colour returned to normal could she relax.

'He said it's up to me entirely how I deal with it but if thoughts of sex overwhelmed me there was something I could do about it once and for all!'

She laughed as if this were some monstrous joke but then stopped short.

'He's right, there is!'

'Liam. Liam!' and she sank back on the bed, shocked. 'Are you talking about being celibate? No sex forever and a day? You?' and she laughed.

'There's a way to make sure, you know. No sex forever and a day!' His eyes were burning and the smile left her face.

'Shit, Liam. You can't mean what I think you mean. That's so contradictory for one thing. The Pastor's been encouraging us on the one hand to be free, and on the other hand he's saying things like that to you. It doesn't make sense.

'And anyway, you wouldn't, you couldn't do anything so crazy!' Her voice had risen in disbelief. 'I mean, my God, Liam, you wouldn't do something like that?'

He stared down at her unflinchingly and nodded his head slowly, yes!

'Then he is mad. And you are mad!' she told him firmly. 'Madder than I ever knew!'

He slapped her face so hard she fell back on the bed, recoiling from him. But he grabbed her shoulders and shook her convulsively. 'Why can't you see? Why can't you hear?' Liam demanded. Words she'd wanted to shriek at *him* over and over these past weeks. 'Why don't you let him save you, save us? Why? Why? Why?' His words were like blows, his grip vice-like. When he finally let her go she didn't speak, just lay there staring at the ceiling, exhausted, sad. Nona felt empty, as if something had ended. He walked to the window then back to the bed, looking down at her. Their eyes met. His expression had changed again.

'You're right, Nona. I couldn't do that,' he began. 'There's no way, even though I want to please the Master so much. I'm too weak, you're right. I'm a coward!' He sat down beside her.

'That's not weakness, Liam, that's your strength! Not giving in to a stupid self-destructive idea like that.' In this instant she knew, if he was not relenting a little, he was having second thoughts. Not coming back but at least turning around. She knew because he grasped her now with a fervour that had nothing to do with the Pastor or his Life Strategies.

'Nona,' he murmured burying his face in her hair.

'Where are you, Liam?' she whispered, filled with pity for him. 'For God's sake, where are you?'

'I'm in hell, that's where.'

'Then don't stay there, come back,' she entreated him.

For full moments they clung together but voices rose up from the rooms below, in the hall a piano played and a choir began a tuneful chant. Then once again, she felt him drawing away from her.

'I'd better go now,' he told her quietly.

'Why? Where are you going?'

'There was to be the Act of Purification tonight. I can't take part. But I need to talk to him.'

'Liam, Liam, you don't have to.'

'I shouldn't be telling you but somehow I want you to understand this, more than anyone else on earth. He's putting all his energies, all his powers into helping me atone for what I did. Helping me save myself. And save young Benny's soul! And again and again I disappoint him. He's helping me, Nona, or trying to, and I just keep letting him down.'

'How?' She had to hear from his own lips what was tearing Liam apart right now, though she knew before he spoke what the guts of it would be. He was silent.

'How are you letting him down?' she asked gently.

'He goes by his dreams—spiritual communions he calls them. He says he's had a recurring dream since arriving in this place six months ago. We worked it out—it's about me. There's a ritual sacrifice can save him. Save my brother Benny. And I can enter this church then for life.'

'Save him or you?' Her heart gave a curious lurch at the word sacrifice.

'Both. Benny and me. He said both of us.'

'At the Devil's Gullet?'

'Yes, but how did you—?'

'I've seen all the boys down there with him in the afternoons. I guessed something was going on. We never meet there any more.' She looked into his eyes.

'You shouldn't be there—'

'I shouldn't be here!'

He smiled at her, a boy again, eager. She stroked his hair.

'I'll be free then, Nona, can't you see?' He wanted her acquiescence, her approval. He seemed to need it. 'I'll be free at last! No more nightmares that drive me to distraction. No more guilt. He said I'd feel renewed. I need that, I really need that.' There were tears in Liam's eyes.

But there'll be another guilt, maybe worse, she wanted to say. Tread softly, something said to her, over and over in her head. 'Sure Liam, I can see that it's important to you,' she soothed.

'We've got to find the Stranger with the Sea Soul. He says there will be signs from the Stranger. He could be here among us all of the time but that he won't be one of us. He'll try to be and fail...and we offer the Stranger to the gods.'

'Offer? In what way?' She hoped he couldn't hear her heart beat as her dread mounted.

'That little ritual for Benny, you know the one we had throwing the wreaths in the pool, in memory of him—the one I started?' He was frowning and she remembered him time and again fighting back tears over his dead brother. This immeasurable guilt he carried.

'Well, the Pastor said I knew instinctively to do that

because it was all in readiness for his coming here. That without knowing it we were already communing spiritually.'

'You mean the wreaths I made were something to do with the Pastor?' She had to control the revulsion she felt at the thought. The loving gathering of shells and flowers and the plaiting of the wire she'd done time and again for the love of Liam. To try to help ease the pain he felt.

'Yes, exactly. He says we were fashioning a ritual for the real sacrifice. Celebrating it. That the way I had the boys making the dive was part of it too. Only I didn't know it consciously. A ritual sacrifice, in readiness for the real thing.'

He didn't need to say it twice. This was madness, mad talk. But Nona knew she must hear every detail, all of it.

'There's a Stranger in our midst, the voice told him. The dive. The Stranger has to make the dive.' His face was shining as he told her. 'Go to the cavern where Benny died. The place where I murdered my brother, the exact same place.'

No point telling him that Benny drowned, that Benny made the dive of his own accord, that no murder had been committed at all, that a boyish hope of impressing a big brother had been the cause of this death. That the boy misjudged the tides completely.

'Where they'll die?' she asked. 'Where the Stranger will die too?'

Liam said nothing for a moment, frowning, not liking to hear the words out in the open. And then he said, 'That's in God's hands.'

'When is it to be made, this dive? Soon?'

He nodded. 'We've been in serious training.'

'So that's what he was up to—' she stopped when Liam frowned. 'That's what you were all doing...'

'Midday tomorrow at the exact time when Benny made the dive for me. Three years ago to be exact. We'll be making one for him, you see.'

'It was high tide then, wasn't it?' Her voice was urgent. 'And isn't it high tide midday? So it's not exactly in God's hands.'

'Ahhh Nona, but it is. Don't you see?' There was a manic light in his eyes she knew too well.

'Ahhh yes,' she echoed, nodding slowly. 'Of course!' She felt sick to the stomach now.

'Who's going to do this dive then? Who's the Stranger, Liam? Does the Pastor think it could be me for instance?' Perhaps this was why he was encouraging her here, she thought in panic.

He laughed at this. 'You, Nona? The Pastor's talking about a boy! Only a male can take part in something like this!'

'Well, there are some benefits to the Pastor's sexist regime,' she wanted to say, but bit back her comment.

'Then who?'

'We're to be guided in a decision. But I can't say the name when I know it, not even to you. All I know is that when it does come to me, he said it will be right!'

Nona nodded and began dressing slowly, thoughtfully.

'So I better go and see him, talk to him,' Liam was saying.

'Yes, you'd better do that.'

'And you won't tell—'

'No, I won't say anything about it.'

'And you'll wait here?'

'I'll stay.'

Not so manic, she thought, that he didn't lock the door after him. Not so manic he didn't find some room for doubt about her, and rightly so. She pushed up the window surveying the way to the ground from the second storey of the old hotel. But Liam wasn't thinking straight because she'd come to his room once before by way of the old drainpipe.

Liam was lost, she concluded as she put her foot over the window sill, brainwashed so expertly that there was no way she could find to reach him. But she could get home to her mother and to Rod. She'd tell them this fantastic Stranger in their Midst story while there was still time.

When she reached the gate she found not one padlock but two. Who had locked the gates? She'd been free to come and go up till now. Everyone had. Even an hour before. She looked up to the high loops of new barbed wire loping about on the freshening breeze. Some handiwork had been going on here that she hadn't noticed before. She turned back to the old hotel. Perhaps one of the men or the women there on kitchen duty would get the keys for her. But something told her not to ask. She felt the desperation and the watchfulness of a convict.

She waited, shivering with cold in the shadows until someone at last approached the gate. It was the Pastor and he had the keys. When the gates were propped open Liam appeared and she saw the Pastor, arm around the young man, turn toward the hill and the church.

'Lock them?' Liam asked.

'We'll only be a short time. No need just yet.'

They were going up there to plot and plan their terrible deed, she was sure. To make it official and 'holy'. She watched them go and, for a few long, bleak minutes felt that love had, at that moment, walked out of her life. Then Nona headed for home.

FOURTEEN

On the way Nona met Rod battling through the wind.

'He's gone crazy. Liam has. Mad as the Pastor!' and she began to cry, as much for Liam as for herself.

'Where is he, Nona?'

'It's no use, the Pastor has this hold over him. It's terrible. They're at the church right now.'

'You better go home. Mum's worried about you. She wants us to leave here tomorrow. You better help her pack.'

'We can't leave! The Pastor's talking crazy. I reckon he's going to make Liam do something dreadful.'

'What do you mean dreadful?'

'He's talking about sacrifice. They've been in secret training. It all sounds ridiculous I know, but Liam's absorbing every word, every idea, dead set! It's going to happen tomorrow!'

'Sandy was on about that, days ago. I better find Liam, have it out with him, once and for all!'

'He won't listen to you. He's changed—completely. He won't even see you!'

But Rod turned to face the hill where the already partly lit church loomed above them.

'I'm coming with you,' Nona insisted and he knew there was no use arguing.

■

'Wait here and keep a lookout,' he told her and she leant against the newly braced timbers of the church. 'I know where I can probably crawl inside. And one inside this place is definitely enough!'

'Door's open,' she told him. 'You can walk in!'

It was true, the doors were open. He heard voices. They were up there in the sacristy, his former friend Liam and the mad Pastor. He had to hear what they were saying. He trod carefully all the way up to the altar where, from above, even in the semi-darkness, the Pastor's photographs seemed to look down on him with a sneer. He went as far as the pulpit, now draped in purple, keeping himself out of sight of the door. With the slightest movement he could see into the small side room.

There were candles, rows of them, burning in there. There was a tall figure sitting on the couch and it was obviously the Pastor. He saw the shock of sandy-coloured hair, the Pastor's fine chiselled features, heard the voice placating someone. He felt a tremor of fear, a choking feeling and wanted to back off immediately. Instead Rod swallowed,

breathed slowly and evenly the way he'd shown Vaughan,
as if for a practice dive. Made himself stay put.

'No, my boy, you are not the one chosen to sacrifice
yourself. I've asked for wisdom about this, we've prayed
together. You know as well as I do it is not the Cherished
Spirits' plan for you at all. You have much more important
work to do now that we have found each other.'

Rod saw the outline of a figure kneeling. Liam, kneeling
before the Pastor. He felt sick at the sight.

'But I know that's what they want,' Liam's voice was
tense with unshed tears. 'I know it'll make it all right again.
I've always known something had to be done.'

'Listen to me. Just listen,' and the Pastor put out his
hand, caressing the shoulder of the young man kneeling
there. 'You've always known there had to be atonement.
Yes, you are right in that. A completion if you will. And you
have to take part in that. But not to give yourself as sacrifice for your brother. The command I hear is very different
indeed.'

'What then?' Liam asked.

'It's a sacrifice as you've always believed. Only a sacrifice
will avenge the death, appease the furies in your mind and
out and around you. You are right. But it's not to be you.
Not you, Liam.'

Rod heard Liam's breathing even from here.

'But—'

'We are going to sit here and meditate together,' the
Pastor interrupted any of his doubts. 'Side by side in this
holy place as I've directed you, and concentrate and ask for
wisdom. And it will come to you. A name will come to us
tonight, and if it does come at one and the same time, as

I know full well it will, then we will know who is the chosen one for the holy sacrifice. We'll both know. Are you prepared?'

Rod hated the way Liam reacted, whispering dutifully, 'Yes, yes of course I am.'

Liam! Revulsion, horror, even laughter welled up in Rod as he listened to the silence. That he could be so taken in with all this Pastor-speak, with the man's holy honeyed tones.

'Don't force it. Just wait for the thought, the face to present itself.'

A silence. Rod's heart beat heavily as fear gathered.

'Wait! I'm feeling something strange, it's getting stronger. Perhaps, just perhaps, it's someone quite new to the Settlement,' the Pastor began again.

What was he doing forcing the choice so obviously like this? Why was Liam playing right into his hands?

'Someone whose actions can save your soul and free your brother's spirit. A boy who does not fit in here at all. Yes, perhaps someone new to the place. Someone with a strong spirit who does not believe. Will not believe. Refuses to hear...a strong spirit that must be at base a bad spirit...'

For a moment Rod thought he might hear his own name.

'You must have that name. Concentrate, concentrate my boy, and it will come to you. Concentrate...and now, now, now...'

A terrible silence.

'Vaughan,' Liam was croaking as if waking up from a dream and then together the two voices named the name, 'Vaughan Roberts.'

Liam jumped to his feet, 'Vaughan Roberts! Vaughan Roberts!' he yelled, his voice filled with joy. The Pastor echoed the shouts.

'Vaughan Roberts. Oh Vaughan Roberts, you are revealed to us at last!'

'Pretty bloody obvious!' Rod wanted to yell in anger. The Pastor wanted someone small and helpless, without a family to defend him. No parents and an old woman who was easily fooled. Vaughan Roberts revealed. What rubbish! He watched as Liam knelt and pressed his lips to the Pastor's hand. He was kissing the Pastor's hand. Oh my God. Rod turned away.

'There, my boy,' the Pastor's voice was gentle, 'there, it wasn't so hard now was it? It came out quite naturally as I thought it would, this night of nights. The Cherished Spirits have spoken. There there, now don't cry. Only the Inner Circle will ever know anything of this. They will be part of the cleansing dive. And it will be the final dreadful and wonderful part of their initiation.'

'We can help you make it come to pass. And you, you can be ordained then as a High Priest. We'll truly be a brotherhood then with only two or three of your Nooan boys to come over. We'll encourage them with your help. And as I've promised you, we will all meet again, soon, very soon with your brother. Tomorrow he will be a Cherished Spirit at last and you are absolved!'

Liam was sobbing now, like a baby. 'Here sit down beside me. It's all right, just sit down a moment by me and I'll comfort you.'

He could burst in there and surprise them. But would that really make Liam see the fakery, the horror? Rod's own eyes were filled with tears of disappointment, surprise and despair. Liam had been his friend. They'd shared everything. The swims, the laughs, the conversations of despair, the deep weight on Liam's soul about Benny. But he'd never mentioned any need for sacrifice. Ritual yes, they'd all been part of the ritual. He'd gone along with that for Liam's sake, because some dark force, some demon of Liam's drove him to try to make amends for Benny. Rod and the other boys had tried to understand that. But in humouring Liam, he and the others must have unwittingly been feeding this other demon desire. Desire for sacrifice.

Rod hadn't realised in their dives, in their desperate little club, that Liam was *waiting* for failure. Waiting for someone to be given up for Benny. Because he could no longer make his own way through the dark tunnel, he wanted someone else to take his place, hoping that their failure to make the dive would be his release. Believing that only then would Benny's death be avenged.

And now the two in there with their so-called Inner Circle were going to aid and abet others in a monstrous act. It was an act that would bind the Inner Circle together for life and that's what the Pastor wanted. Simple as that.

Rod had heard it with his own ears. A sacrifice. He began to edge away from the two in there, away from the altar that was despoiled by that imposter's voice, by his calling as any kind of spiritual leader.

Where in the hell was Vaughan Roberts right now? Where was Father James right now? He'd phone the old priest and try to tell him what was going on in his own church under the guise of goodness. But what could Father James or Father anyone do so far from what was happening here? What was *about* to happen. No, they must get through to the Cat Harbour police to stop all this.

He trod softly back down the aisle and out into the night air, taking deep breaths as if he'd just emerged from some cold underwater swim himself. He felt almost blinded by the white light of the moonlit sandy street.

They'd get the hell out of town as fast as they could and take Vaughan with them. They wouldn't wait until tomorrow. The car was packed. He'd break in and pinch the fuel somehow. To hell with saying goodbye to Liam. It wasn't Liam in there any more but some blathering puppet of the Pastor's.

'Well?' Nona was beside him in a moment.

'Liam named Vaughan Roberts,' he said, still amazed by what had transpired, 'to do an impossible high tide dive tomorrow!'

'Vaughan Roberts! Good God!' Nona looked stunned. 'And I think they really mean him to do it!'

'Of course they bloody do. I've got to find him.'

They sped down the hill and through the night, two shadows slipping into darkness as the lights in the church were extinguished behind them. But once well away Nona slowed, grabbed her brother's arm, stopped dead.

'You find him, I'm going back to the Compound,' she told him.

'You can't,' he caught hold of her hand. 'They're bloody well plotting murder up there. Can't you understand? We've got to—'

She wrenched her hand free and he saw the tears streaming down her face. 'I've got to go back. Try to see him, tell him I'm going. Try to talk him into coming with us.'

'Nona, that's not possible! Don't tell them we're leaving. that would be mad!'

'Well, I've got to at least see him. I know he's taking part in all this but for God sake's, Rod, he's deluded. Someone's got to try to get through to him.' She was running through the darkness and he knew there was no way he could catch her.

Rod turned into the main road. There was that strange feeling he'd known before, that the laden sandhills were moving, rolling forward bit by bit, rolling forward to overtake the town. He was spooked, but tried to reason that it was a person trying to take over. The town, the place was impartial. Yet, when he passed by the Vees' place, those thrusting stones glinting in the moonlight seemed even more malevolent tonight. Maybe they're on the Pastor's side, he thought wildly.

He trudged on, thinking over the conversation he'd heard. What in the hell had the Pastor meant when he said 'And as I've promised you we will all meet again, soon, very soon with your brother'? That was a worry for sure.

When he turned the corner into their street, Rod could see his mother's figure through the blinds at their place. She was pacing agitatedly. And when he drew near he could see why. The car! There was not one flat tyre, but four of them!

'What the hell?' he sped indoors. He could see she'd been crying.

'I came back from the town this afternoon—everyone I met acting so bloody strange. I went to see if the public phones were working. And when I got back here somebody had done this. Rod, I'm scared!'

He gave her a hug. Thought she might collapse. Told her exactly what he'd heard at the church.

'I knew it. I knew the man was mad from day one. We've got to get out now and you're right, we have to take Vaughan with us. But how?'

'Tyres can be mended, Mum. Fuel can be got and so can Vaughan. We'll do it.'

'Where's Nona?'

He didn't need to tell her. Already she'd jumped up and was pulling on her coat. 'I'm sick to death of all this. I'm going over there to get her myself!'

'You can't. Not right this minute. We've really got to think all of this through.' He was amazed at his own sanity.

'I've had enough! He's not taking over Nona! I'm going to face that Pastor and ask him directly about this crazy idea of his. Talk to people over there and tell them just what's going on with Vaughan and with our family. They can't all be—'

'No!' he yelled at her. 'No, it won't make any difference. You're dealing with madness. And you of all people know what that's all about!' He might have hit her for she stopped in her tracks.

'I'm sorry, Ma. I know it's not the same thing as it was with Dad but it is a madness. It's like a virus over there, a shared obsession, mania, delusion. Call it what you will but it's a form of madness. Everyone's sharing it right now. And you can't, you just can't single-handedly deal with it. There's no one left who's able to face up to him. Please, I know what I'm talking about, I've just heard him...heard them...I know...'

She turned back. 'But I've got to try to do something.'

'I do have an idea. I think it'll get us through, get Nona out of there. Being reasonable won't, Mum.'

She came back and sat down on the bulging armchair. For a moment he thought she'd collapse but he saw her square her shoulders.

'What is it?'

'We have to be as tricky as he is. I still have an easy entry to the Compound. So does Nona, come to that. They want us there. He does. It's all his ego, to gather in the last resisting ones. And especially the doubting teacher. That would demonstrate his power! Same way as he's getting the Nooan boys one by one. Don't you see?'

She was tense but was listening to every word as if he'd solve everything, and hell, he wasn't even sure...

'So what if I go over and play along with it? And in the meantime you get things ready here. Sit out the night. Go to Mr Clemens in the morning for the petrol, have the tyres mended. Hint you're thinking of going over to the Compound in the next few days. That'll get around pretty quick. And it'll keep us mobile.'

He saw her white tense face. 'You go over there?'

'Mum, it's our only way. Otherwise they'll keep Nona and God knows what will happen!' He didn't want to mention the worrying 'we'll all meet again soon' bit to his mother but it made his own stomach clench. 'I've got to get to Vaughan somehow.'

'You can't save the world you know, Rod!' she said, 'You should think of Nona first and then—'

'We'll be out of here tomorrow with Nona and Vaughan, Mum! Both of them!'

'Wish I could feel so confident,' she said.

'Let's make a meeting place and a time and if we don't front then you go and get help.'

'It all sounds so desperate. I can't let you, I really can't,' she said. 'It wouldn't be right. And the risk involved—no!'

'There's risk sitting here doing nothing. And to walk out for help...well, we could, but that's two days isn't it? And in the meantime...'

She gave in at the end. There seemed no alternative. 'I'll keep on trying the phone in town,' she said, 'but I'm not hopeful! And yes, I'll get the petrol first thing.'

They confirmed a meeting place near Madshark, in case Rod didn't get back tonight. He reiterated, 'I'm going to *try* to stay there, go along with them.' And then he was at the door. 'Nona and Vaughan, Mum. Out of here for sure!' And she gave him a worried half-smile before he took off into the darkness.

FIFTEEN

The evening would be long, Vaughan thought. In the morning, at very first light, maybe even a bit before first light, he'd get out. He'd walk direct across the sandhills, find the main road and get to the next town some way, hitch a ride maybe. Something weird was happening here, something he felt building up to a climax and he knew he didn't want to be part of it.

Well, thank God Fishface hadn't thought to turn off the electricity! Not yet! Vaughan settled in front of the television, a metallic aftertaste from the tinned spaghetti in his mouth.

When the phone rang it was like a jet of black sound across the room. The Pastor? One of his henchmen? He stood up uncertain. Or maybe, just maybe—and he didn't know why he thought of it because she never ever phoned—maybe his mum? He grabbed the receiver, ready to smash it down again should the wrong voice be on the other end.

'How you doin', mate?'

Disappointment at no prolonged signals indicating an overseas call and then relief. It was Rod's voice. 'I thought you might be gone?'

'Tried to, mate, but some bastard's slashed our tyres, would you believe? I'm at the public phone too. What's happening your end?'

'My gran's gone over there. This afternoon.'

'Yeah, well whole town has looks like...'

'Shit!'

'Yeah, everyone excepting thee and me!'

'What's that?'

'And the walls have ears, mate.' He was on a public phone but he was still nervous.

'Can I see you?' Vaughan asked, suddenly feeling like a little boy. There was a long pause

'Lonely Place?' Rod suggested curtly.

'Now?'

'Yeah.'

As he made his way through the wind, missing the one woolly jumper his gran must have packed and taken with her, he hoped the bulky figure leaning against the timber shelter at the end of the wharf was Rod's.

'Didn't want to advertise,' Rod spoke from the shadows.

'Sure.'

Rod looked deadly serious in the half-light as he let them into the tiny room that smelled of wetsuits and oils and fish and a summer already almost over.

'What's cooking?' Vaughan asked, grateful to see this

familiar face once again. Rod was shaking his head as he motioned Vaughan to sit on the pile of fishnets in one corner. He looked out the window before he too sat down.

'Things look a bit grim!' Rod said.

'Yeah? What's up?' Vaughan tried to sound normal but his voice was hoarse.

'There's some mad talk I've heard about a ritual for the sea tomorrow. It'll save Liam's soul and a few others as well.'

Vaughan cleared his throat. 'I don't get it. Ritual? D'you mean the dive or what?'

'Nona's over there with Liam right now. She's the only one allowed in and out of that place. And she's come back to tell me things our mum suspected about that crazy man. And tonight I heard for myself. In the church. Plain as day,' he smiled here, 'even though it was night, mate.' Then his face became serious again. 'Worse than I imagined. Bloody crazy things!'

The wind was wheeling round the shed and sitting there with Rod, Vaughan felt an apprehension that made him straighten his back, as if to withstand the news Rod brought.

'Yes?'

'Sandy was acting stoolie for me, telling me things when he could, but I reckon the Pastor's got him fingered now. He was s'posed to meet me and never came back again. I told you the bastard locks the kids up. Anyway, haven't seen Sandy in a while to ask what's happening there. But now I know!'

'Go on.' Vaughan wondered why Rod had chosen the

deserted jetty to tell him all this...and why he was taking so long about it.

'I heard something between Liam and the Pastor, and it was about you!'

'About me?' It was like a blow and yet he knew it was coming, had been coming, forever. As soon as Rod said 'about you', those fateful words, he knew it! Recognised it as the source of the unaccountable fear he'd felt on first arriving in this town. As if it had always been there, the something, waiting to pounce. He tried to swallow back some of that gaping fear but even though Rod was here beside him, and he looked to Rod as some sort of protector, it was impossible.

'Mum's been trying to make long distance calls but she couldn't. Phones are still working in the town but we reckon they've been tinkered with. Reckon they're listening. That's why I couldn't say—'

'What did they say about me?' Vaughan felt like a little kid reaching out for his dad's hand in the darkness.

'Tomorrow—maybe even tonight—they'll come and get you. Take you over there.'

'That wasn't the deal.'

'No time left for a deal. Anyway, who's making deals with you?'

'A letter from him. I found it at home,' Vaughan told him.

'And you trust him? C'mon. Like I said, no time. It's the anniversary tomorrow.'

'I should know? Whose?' Rod seemed to be talking in riddles and maybe he didn't want them untangled.

'Benny's death in the Devil's Gullet. Liam's brother's

death. The one he feels so guilty about! The one the Pastor's using so cleverly.'

Benny! That name again. So that was it, the wreaths and the ritual dive. Well, what was it to do with him? Or the Pastor for that matter? Then the dream rose up in his memory, that underwater dream and the young boy's face with the blood streaming from his mouth. God no! How could Benny, a boy he didn't even know, a boy he didn't know anything about, enter his dreams?

'Nona heard them say a stranger was going to be the centrepiece of some spooky sacrafice he's cooked up to get allegiance—I don't know—get *something* from all those boys. I heard them naming you. To do the dive, at midday.'

'But I couldn't, I mean I'm not ready to make the dive now. I haven't practised for weeks.'

'They're not worried about that.'

'But they can't make a person...'

Vaughan stared into Rod's eyes. In the moonlight he could read something there he didn't want to know. Rod was nodding his head slowly. 'They can...and it just happens to be high tide...'

'Shit!' Vaughan's voice was loud.

'I'd get going if I were you, right now. Not by the road either. Go across the hills. Keep the road in sight but don't walk on it.' He saw the terror welling in Vaughan's eyes. 'If you do that it'll be okay. And we'll try to meet you tomorrow. Mum and Nona and me. We'll be leaving soon as we can.'

'I'd be a target out there in the moonlight, wouldn't I?' The night seemed to be shining in the window, a bright enemy. Rod shook his head.

'Worse here for you. Take some water though. Gets hot as hell out there in the day.'

He wanted to say, 'I don't want to go alone. Why don't you come with me?' but he was silent.

Rod must have guessed the consternation the younger boy felt. 'I got a few things to do before we leave. Snitch some new tyres for one. Go *find* Nona for another. Talk her into leaving Liam.'

'A boat?' Vaughan's voice was hopeful. He could go right now by boat.

'The ones out there on the beach are busted. Been down to check the lot of them and their fishing boats. They've chained the whole damn lot together on the beach. Chained them so no one can use them without a key! We gotta go by the road.' Rod rose and looked out the window as if checking out the landscape. 'This place, I don't know, it gives me the willies. Even the bloody rocks out there!

'Listen mate, you can start walking.' He turned back, the old Rod, confident, encouraging. 'We'll pick you up tomorrow out at Five Mile.'

'But I don't even know where Five Mile is.'

'You came through Five Mile to get here. Must have. It's nothing but a busted-up petrol station in the middle of desert. Wait there for us. And if we don't turn up for any reason you're fit enough to do a two-day walk! Long as you have your water. And long as you bring the police back here straight away. Just keep heading south, okay.'

He patted Vaughan's arm encouragingly for the boy looked dazed. 'It'll be okay as long as you get clear of here tonight,' Rod told him.

Vaughan smiled a wan appreciation of all this news. He wondered why Rod's voice sounded so unconvincing when he added, 'Piece of cake, mate. Piece of cake!'

SIXTEEN

'I've come to see my sister,' he said as soon as he found Liam.

Rod had walked to the gates, calling out to a man inside to have them opened. There'd been no trouble getting in. And no trouble finding Liam. It seemed almost all too easy, though he was aware the gates were locked behind him. Some haven, he thought.

'Sure. She's here somewhere.' Liam spoke reasonably, seeming his old self for a moment despite the long, flowing purple robes he was wearing. Rod hadn't been prepared for the emotion he felt face to face with Liam again, despite what he'd heard at the church and from Nona.

They walked through the old hotel entrance together and beyond that into the large, green palm courtyard. But something about the way Liam walked beside him, the way he held himself so upright, draped in those robes, seeming just like the Pastor, annoyed Rod. He couldn't hold back.

'Haven't seen you since you came here,' he began.

'I sent word to you to come too. You're welcome any time. I told you that! I kept expecting you. Still do,' Liam answered.

Sure, Rod thought, they'd had their one brief and unsatisfactory meeting. 'My stakes gone up or what?' he joked.

Liam had an unreadable expression on his face but Rod felt a compulsion to pursue the conversation, looking for some kind of breakthrough. They were alone for one thing, though he saw figures moving constantly on the upper verandahs. A to and fro of people, unnervingly quiet.

'I wanted the chance to talk to you,' Rod began. 'I'm hearing things, a few strange things.'

'Yeah?' The two stood facing each other. All around them the warm lights of the old hotel rooms were making the palm leaves glow gold, throwing great pools of amber on the grass. It felt like a film set to Rod. Difficult to believe the tall, healthy-looking youth had anything planned for tomorrow that was not normal, even wholesome. Difficult to believe that a man he'd known scarcely six months was controlling this person so absolutely.

Liam was smiling and encouraging. 'Like what?' he asked.

Don't fall into the trap, Rod thought, tempted to pour it all out. But maybe this was the moment to try to get through to his old friend. 'Don't you think,' he began awkwardly, treading carefully as Nona had earlier, 'don't you think this Pastor's a bit of a control freak. Wants control over everyone?'

'You're wrong there.' Liam smiled politely, spoke politely

as if to a worrisome child. 'Look, the Pastor's a miracle worker. He's not controlling them. He's *saving* them, saving all of us. And that's the truth.' It was as if a wall of glass was descending between them again.

'I just don't get it!' Rod shook his head. 'Why doesn't everyone just go to the church? Why come over here to live?'

'The Settlement's long since gone bust. It was only a matter of time before it was a ghost town. Maybe weeks if he hadn't come. Now there's hope for everyone again. That's why they've come over here. He gives them hope.'

'You mean for everyone who wants to go his way, do his thing,' Rod insisted.

'Sure, and what's so bad about his way?'

'Everyone seems,' he paused then rushed on, 'well, they seem bloody hypnotised.'

'Listen, mate, you can't hypnotise three hundred people now, can you? They made choices. Simple as that. They wanted a new life. They wanted direction and yes, they want to be directed, too. Look, I want to show you something.'

They walked through the courtyard and out through the archway. He saw plot after plot of thriving vegetables.

'This was a wasteland, you remember. Cinders and sand. It's an oasis now. But this isn't all.'

Beyond the vegetable gardens he saw the old glasshouses all mended and sparkling with new paint. And beyond that again the fishing boats he'd checked only an hour before. They were no longer hopelessly straggling along the beach, every which way as they had for years. They were in neat lines, scraped and fresh-looking again, obviously being put to good use. So why did he think of chicken guts, excrement, blood?

'He likes order and he brings order to the whole place. To people.' Liam spoke so proudly. 'Some of the kids don't like it at first. He's pretty strict with them. Has to be. But you begin to see the sense of order in everything, adults too—even in the way you eat a meal or sweep a floor. He's big on rules for everything.'

Rod had noticed the gleaming tiles in the hotel foyer, had seen colours lost maybe fifty years ago to grime. But was that really so great? And why should someone tell a grown person how to sweep or how to eat a meal?

Singing rose up from a room nearby, sweet voices, a song of joy.

'Listen to that,' and Liam was smiling again. 'You can't *make* people sound like that. They're happy, mate. What's wrong with that?'

Liam threw his arm round Rod's shoulders in a familiar gesture as they walked back through the courtyard. 'I've been waiting to show you all this. You're my mate, you know that.'

'But it's not the same,' Rod told him, strangely repulsed by his tone.

'Only if you don't want it to be,' Liam answered smoothly.

'I can't say what I really want to say to you.'

For the first time Liam's eyes met his. 'Sure you can! It's been the biggest change in my life, I feel...hey look, Rod, I just wish you could share this with us. I feel like I can be free again. I feel like there's hope for the first time since...since...'

'I know.'

'Yeah, since Benny. And it's to do with him, the Pastor. That weird guy I used to laugh at and mock. We both did. I've told him everything. Even the names we used to call him.'

'Shit, mate, why?'

'He said I should come clean. To the bone he said, and I wanted to.'

'But he's not a Father Confessor.'

'Why not?' Liam's voice had an edge again. 'He's been totally honest and open with me so why shouldn't I reciprocate?' He had pulled a little away from Rod but still confided in him. 'Listen to me, mate, that man's shared my nightmares. Taken them on his own shoulders. He's cried for me and with me. It's...it's bloody amazing.' Liam's eyes were shining now. 'And I don't want to let him down. Only I do. In so many ways I do!'

Rod stopped interrupting and trying to reason. He let Liam recount what he wanted with all his new found ardour. In the meantime his eyes kept glancing up to the windows. Nona must be up there somewhere.

'And he's in touch with the dead. With Benny. Same as I will be!' He saw the look on Rod's face. 'Yeah, I knew that'd shock you.'

Rod realised then, as he looked into the smiling face, that he'd probably never find the old Liam. The real Liam. And nor would Nona. Or maybe the rhapsodic youth before him, who had been absolved of all real responsibility, was after all the real Liam.

'Look, I'd better go see Nona,' Rod turned away but Liam touched his arm lightly.

'You think I'm crazy but if you'd just come to one of the meetings, you'd understand. Stay just one night. Tonight! It'd change your life. Give it a try?'

Rod was about to give a curt no but remembered this was why he'd come. This was his big chance. 'Yeah, maybe,' Rod said cautiously, as if considering it a moment while his mind worked furiously. He saw the flicker of triumph on Liam's face and felt sick. 'But first I want Nona to come home to see Mum.'

Liam's expression changed, his whole manner. 'Nona may not want to leave here, thought of that?' He seemed to be challenging Rod.

'I'd like to ask her, mate,' Rod kept his tone reasonable.

'This is her family now,' Liam said triumphantly. Not Liam but the Pastor's boy now. 'And there's not a thing you can do about it! Her family's here.'

At this moment, despite all his intentions, Rod felt the desire to punch the fatuous, Pastor-like face in front of his. He had to control his rage.

'Where's my sister?'

'She's not your sister! You told me she was adopted so she's just as much anyone's sister, if it comes to it!'

'Don't be crazy. Nona *is* my sister!'

'She's made her choice, same as me,' Liam taunted. 'She's not part of your family any more. So get that into your skull, thickhead, once and for all!'

That did it. Rod threw a punch and they were on the ground before he could even think about it. He felt a mad rage of desire to shake it out of the person who'd been his friend, beat out this brainwashed drivel he'd had to suffer. Rod was bigger and heavier but Liam was wiry and strong.

They were all too evenly matched. But when Liam's nose spurted blood Rod came to his senses, rose to his feet and made off through the corridor calling for his sister. He'd blown it for sure! He'd have to find her and get out of here! And they'd damn well follow Vaughan across the sandhills by foot, if they had to.

He ran up the stairs as if pursued, calling, frantic. People stopped in corridors looking at him askance. And then he saw the Pastor himself hurrying towards him.

'What's all this fuss, my boy? Your sister's in here talking to me!' Reasonable, concerned, friendly. He was in a madhouse. The Pastor led Rod straight into a large pleasant room lined with books, a pleasant room. But then he saw the pictures and posters of the Pastor above the shelves, on every spare piece of wall. A kinder looking, younger and more thoughtful Pastor. But the eyes were the same eyes that had looked down on him in the church. The coldness in them could not be hidden. Rod looked directly into those same eyes now.

'We don't allow any violence in the Home of the Church of the Most Cherished Spirits you know. That's a rule.' So he'd seen the fight down there. Yet he was speaking in such a reasonable voice. Rod wanted to laugh at that voice, to remind him of the beatings he'd heard about or the welts on Sandy's back that he'd seen with his own eyes but Nona spoke first. He had to control his surprise.

'I've decided to stay for tonight's meeting, Rod, and I think you should too.' Her voice seemed to come from far away. But there she was, sitting comfortably in one of the big armchairs. She seemed quite at home. The thought crossed his mind that the Pastor or someone there may have drugged her!

'I told the Pastor you really wanted to join the boys over here all along. Only Mum wouldn't let you. Or me.'

No, she wasn't drugged. Her eyes looked into his. She was smart, his sister, and she was playing the game he'd come to play and hadn't managed at all! *Her* eyes were alive, pleading, cautious all at once.

'I think you should stay for the meeting.' Nona was speaking in that same mild voice that Liam had used from time to time, as if speaking to a child. 'Ring Mum and tell her. I'll go home in the morning. I want to talk her into joining us all over here tomorrow. I've told the Pastor.'

'And I think that sounds a wonderful idea,' the Pastor couldn't hide the satisfaction in his voice. Nona smiled and then added, looking at Rod, 'I might go back to that lonely place. I told the Master that's what we call home these days, such a lonely place now.' She said this slowly and deliberately. 'And I'd go back there if I thought it would *help* someone. But here with friends is better.'

Had she gone mad? What was this about a lonely place? Lonely Place! No she wasn't mad at all. She was perfectly sane and she was talking their code for his scuba dive forays. But what the hell did she mean? 'I might go to the Lonely Place if I thought it would *help* someone.' Ah yes, now he got it. He wanted to smile and nod at her but the Pastor spoke and he was obliged to attend, look into the pale eyes.

'I'm very pleased with your sister,' the Pastor began, motioning Rod to another chair. 'She's been a difficult one there's no doubt. Filled with misgivings. But this evening she's reached a high point in prayer with me, I'm pleased to say. And now I know she's to truly become one of us. As you will be Rodney, I'm sure. Will you take part in a pre-initiation meeting?'

He saw an almost imperceptible nod from Nona, the sign he'd wanted that she was very much in control. And that gave him courage to agree despite his revulsion.

'Yes, I will,' he said.

'Good, good.' The Pastor was actually rubbing his hands. 'You see we may need you to help us.'

'How's that?'

'Vaughan Roberts' grandmother is so upset about her boy. We know that he likes you and will listen to you. You may be able to help us find him and bring him here.' He blinked and dropped his voice. 'We fear though that that young man may have already left town, despite our prayers for him. However, if he can be found...'

'I don't know about that.' He looked over at Nona. Did they have Vaughan already? How could he know? And yet Nona seemed to be indicating...He said to her, 'If you go, Nona, you could fetch necessary things from the Lonely Place,' as if he were referring to their home.

'No need to do that yet. We'll get your things later. But you can be sure, my friends, you'll never be lonely again,' the Pastor said warmly. 'You will find comradeship and a fellowship here you've never dreamed of.'

'I might go home for a bit,' Nona said, so meekly Rod was surprised. 'That is, if it's okay with you, Pastor? I'd like to talk to our mother about coming over here.' But the

Pastor was already enthusing over Rod and merely nodded to her.

'I'm going to show you some very interesting videos about the Cherished Ones and then we're going to talk, Rodney my boy! There's a lot to get through tonight but if you are willing as you say—'

'Yes, I am.'

Go like the wind, Nona, go! he was thinking as he heard his sister's quick footsteps down the stairs.

'I and my companions will take you far into the night. Oh yes, we're going to talk! And we're going to pray. We're going to meditate. And we're going to consider. Then in the morning of an important day for all of us here, we'll be leaving you to a long, and I hope, a refreshing sleep. Step one of the initiation will be complete. And to think your sister and your mother who's been opposing her fate for so long will be here with us at last!'

Rod's eyes took in the sweep of the room, the fact that the windows were small—too small! But hey, he wasn't thinking of escape. Not yet. He should concentrate, go with the tide of Pastor-words.

'But we are fair about everything here. When you wake, young Rodney, you can make up your own mind as to whether you really want to be part of this happy community. As your sister has and your mother can. We're very democratic here as you already know. No one comes and certainly no one stays against their will. You'll be free to go or stay. As Nona is. If you stay, you take the classes that all the young folk here have taken, and in time that will lead to your full initiation. Your mother can undertake a series of courses too. That implies full commitment, of course.'

Rod thought of his mother's response and had a mad impulse to laugh but instead he cleared his throat and nodded sagely.

'If you decide to leave, any of you, well then that's your own business. But I'll be disappointed. We'll all be disappointed. How does that sound then?'

The Pastor was actually smiling at him, showing his small even teeth and the tip, just the tip of his pointed tongue.

Sweet reason. Sweet lies. Rod knew he was looking into a viper's mouth.

'Will you submit?'

Rod hated that word and he had no intention of doing it but he nodded his assent again. He almost panicked at the thought of a night being talked at by the Pastor and his cohorts. What if he lost his mind? His will? He thought of Vaughan Roberts and the sacrificial dive and steeled himself.

The Pastor was as good as his word. He talked and didn't let up for some hours. And then when he'd left the room, no doubt to rest after his energies were somewhat depleted, someone else took over, one of his 'disciples' with the same enthusiasm and energy. It was an orgy of love and devotion and Rod could not distinguish whether it was for the Cherished Spirits (to whom the Pastor had access) or to the Master (who was both an earthly manifestation of a Cherished Spirit and but a simple man—their Pastor).

They went over and over what it meant to belong. The joys and the responsibilities, the hopes and outcomes of the strength of unity, the submergence of the individual for the good of the whole, the control of desires, the adherence to the laws and ultimate strength in complying, the initiation which was the formal recognition of the Pastor as Master. As the night wore on and words and prayers and images and chants whirled through Rod's brain, he found it was hard to hold onto the reason he was here.

Towards the dawn Liam joined him and Rod found himself crying and hugging him and there was no pretence in that. Then the Pastor came back and was hugging both of them and Rod was aware of a great sweeping relief, that it was all over for the time being.

'Thank God you're here to stay,' Liam said over and over, genuinely happy for Rod. And then, as if checking himself, 'Thanks be to the power of the Cherished Spirits.' Rod saw Liam and the Pastor exchange shining glances.

'We all need rest for the ceremony up ahead today,' the Pastor told him. 'You can't be part of this ceremony, Rodney. You are not one of the Inner Circle or even a Cherished One just yet. But in a few more weeks I'm sure you'll be fit. And you say your mother is at last interested? This is wonderful. A whole family together. Good news indeed!'

Rod nodded compliance.

'Take Rodney to his room now, Liam, and let him rest.'

He wanted to stay awake. He wanted to take stock of all that had happened since he'd 'submitted'. Go over the details of all that had transpired in that room. He wanted to shore up the feeble line of resistance he thought still there. He wanted to so much but all Rod remembered when he woke up hours later, was that he'd seen the bed in the small room Liam offered with its fresh sheets, its inviting pillow, and he'd made for it like a drunken man. Then a swift, a beautiful, obliteration.

SEVENTEEN

All the way across the ice blue hills, despite numerous over-the-shoulder glances to check, Vaughan felt as if there were eyes on him. As he came level with the snaking, sandy road he felt sure. He pulled back into the shadow of the hills. He remembered Rod's warning. He'd not go by the road at all but move parallel to it. Too late. They emerged from the shadowland at the other side.

'Goin' somewheres?' It was the butcher's boy.

'What's it to you?'

'Pastor says the road's closed till tomorrow. Said if you showed invite you to come back with us.'

'I don't want to—'

Two of them, young men he did not know, moved in so close he could feel the longing in their fists as they clenched their hands. Maybe they were the Nooan boys? Whatever, they were big and they were strong.

'However, if you insist...' he quipped.

The blow to the side of his head sent him reeling. 'Just walk, smartarse. Walk.'

Their feet crunched out a solemn rhythm on the sandy road. Vaughan walked with careless scraping steps, hoping footprints would tell Rod and his mum, someone, the story! But the incessant wind soon put paid to that idea.

They dumped him in the laundry outhouse at the hotel. The detested place for recalcitrant children, for youths like Sandy Mason, to cool off after their unsuccessful sessions with the Pastor. Dark and windowless, Vaughan could see no escape. There was a mattress on the floor and water from the constantly dripping tap and that was all. A silence. He sat with his back against the wall, concentrating on the slither of light he located under the door. They'd come for him in the morning, he knew that.

He tried to stay awake, alert, but even in his fear he slept a few hours. Must have, for when the door was dragged open the dazzle of morning light shocked him. He shrank back, refusing to be led out but it only made things worse. They ripped off his shirt and then they strong-armed him out of the airless room and across the courtyard. Someone covered his mouth. He could bite on it but there wasn't a person in sight and even if there was, would it help to scream? As they cleared the Compound, the hand was taken away. His foot twisted on the rocky path down to the sea and then he did scream. That was when they began dragging him.

He tried to call out their names, to appeal to them one by one. 'Hey Shane, hey Tom!' the ones he knew. But the sand, when he stumbled, flew up into his eyes, his nostrils, his mouth. And they didn't want to hear. Only one of them spoke directly to him, telling him with a jeering voice that their names had changed.

'I'm Aroo,' he said, 'not Shane, you dickhead!'

'How can your names have changed?' he panted. 'You're bloody Shane Williams and you know it!' A resounding thump on his back from someone in the posse behind him silenced him.

They were pulling him over the volcanic rock now and even the most stalwart of them gave him a break here, a moment to climb to his feet again. But not in time to save his knees that were bloodied on the first contact. They pulled him, stumbling awkwardly, over the rocks and towards the pool. What in the hell was going on? This ritual swim thing the Pastor and Liam had cooked up? Well, he wouldn't be part of it. He wouldn't co-operate at all.

Round the boulder he saw the rest of them. Standing soldier-like, strange divers in their goggles. The sun gleamed unconvincingly carefree, glints of it in his eyes, but the group standing at attention seemed far from carefree.

Then the Pastor stepped out in front of them. His pale eyes were expressionless but Vaughan recognised the unstinting hardness in his whole demeanour—straight-backed, the purple robes flowing in the wind, his pale hair ruffling too.

' "For every evil under the sun",' Vaughan thought at the sight of him.

They stood in two rows—boys he knew and some he'd never seen before. He realised it must have been rehearsed because they were in ascending order of height. In the background he saw the butcher and two other adults he didn't know.

Dyson and another boy arrived carrying what looked like ski bags—bright purple and yellow bags that unzipped to show fishing spears. Dyson, Vaughan noted, never looked his way. The company pulled off their T-shirts and took a spear each. That was when he realised the worst. He saw the frightening uniformity of the purple and yellow symbols emblazoned on their chests and the immobility of their expressions. They were not about to go scuba diving.

The Pastor, in the meantime, had taken up a position on an outcrop of rock higher than the rest. He stared over Vaughan's head and out to sea and began to chant. It was in the kind of monotone easy to ignore except that the Pastor was using the word 'sacrifice'. Yes, and he'd said that word again.

Vaughan searched their faces. Each and everyone of them wore the same ardent look he interpreted as adoration for this man. But suddenly the group turned. Someone else was approaching. Someone, Vaughan hoped, who'd stop this whole terrible charade, this ridiculous farce of a sea sport. Then everyone would act naturally again, the boys he knew fooling and talking together in the old way, saying it was a joke, a trick, a crazy simulation. And he'd be able to fade away from the place and forget he'd ever had the wish to do the dive at all!

Vaughan's heart leapt because he recognised the strong determined face. But surely this wasn't Liam in purple getup just like the Pastor, flowing robes that whipped around him in the wind? It *was* Liam.

'Hey, Liam,' he yelled at once but Liam's eyes were on his Master. Vaughan should run like a madman right now but the butcher, as if anticipating such a move, stepped forward and put a heavy restraining hand on Vaughan's arm. He nodded his head towards the Pastor as if telling Vaughan to attend.

'...and so dear ones, we shall be carried to the mountains of exaltation, to the peaks of excellence if the sea is appeased, the sensuous land is rewarded and the grudging rocks befriended. Especially Brother Liam's secret tabernacle, a saltily sacred place where we know a troubled spirit awaits release.

'We know all too well the seriousness of the undertaking here today. The most dreadful secrecy of it that will bind every man, every boy in a brotherhood as indestructible and good as it is eternal. We know the necessity of releasing the spirit that has been so long trapped beneath our feet, so that this place, the sea here, can prosper again in quite a different way to before. And so that individuals in it can be loving to one another, so that the Master is fully recognised and so that Chosen Ones—in the first instance Brother Liam here—may ascend to the status unblemished of High and Cherished Priest.'

Then he turned slowly, slowly and for the first time his eyes fell on Vaughan.

'A Stranger has been delivered to our midst, as was foretold, a member of his own family bears the acknowledgment of sacrifice in her very name. And he shall leave our midst today as was ordained, through his young and willing efforts.'

A spasm made Vaughan clench his teeth and words were blotted out for the moment as blood pounded noisily through his ears. But he'd heard the word 'willing'.

'I'm not willing,' he shouted in his fury, 'D'you hear? I'm bloody *un*willing!' But the Pastor droned on, his eyes glazed. 'And if he is Chosen, as we believe the Cherished Spirits will choose him, then at his demise his memory shall be hallowed here by every man and every boy, binding us together in brotherhood till the end.'

Demise. Spears glinting now in the sunlight, the motionless enthralled group, the mesmerising evil words. Demise? Shit, he wasn't going to stay another second! Vaughan sprang up the rock in a valiant and useless attempt.

'Oh no you don't!' the butcher broke the spell with a hearty, almost parental chiding, but his strong hands seized the boy and jerked one arm unkindly behind Vaughan's back.

Surely, surely what was about to happen here would not be allowed. What about the other adults present? The butcher was a father. He couldn't go through with this. He looked at the faces of those he knew and at Liam but they all seemed to be sleepwalking. Liam was standing with the others like a dumbbell, staring into space as if Vaughan were not here, or were truly a stranger to him. But as he was led back to his appointed place, Vaughan thought he saw the sweat of fear on Liam's brow. Liam, save me from this. Save me! His eyes were beseeching but Liam continued to stare straight ahead.

■

Rod was roused by the birds. A couple of kookaburras laughing madly in the palms outside the window brought him to consciousness. He saw at once the day was not young. He jumped up in a panic and found the note on the floor. It must have been poked underneath as he slept. He took it with trembling hands and immediately recognised the handwriting.

I've been to the Lonely Place and I've seen Vaughan Roberts down by the sea. He can do the dive.

Nona! Good girl, she'd had the sense to keep up their code. And she was out there somewhere. Never mind, he'd find her. But when he tried the door he found it was locked.

He looked down at his watch for the first time. God, maybe he'd slept through till midday! His heart thumped but it was with relief when he saw it was 11am. Still time to get down there. Time to get down there and do what? Distract them, mislead them, *something*. But get down there fast. Get out of here first.

Rod looked around for a way of escape. But the small room he'd slept in, obviously a former hotel storeroom, was one of the few rooms that had stout bars on the windows. Had they meant to lock him in like this? After all that brotherly, comradely shit last night? He sank down on the bed. Of course they had. He was on the way but he wasn't one of them yet and they had things to do today. Important things. Nona had got to Lonely Place, thank God. But

how could she get to Vaughan? *He* had to, before…Some-
one was just going to have to let him out!

Rod banged on the door, yelling, but the corridor outside was obviously empty. He went back to the window and
looked down onto the palm court. There Rod saw the figures of some women in the kitchen, and then a broader
more familiar figure sweeping the paved area. He recognised Vaughan's grandmother and his heart leapt.

'Mrs Roberts!' he called, trying to sound normal, cheery.
'Hullo down there, Mrs Roberts.'

She looked up, shading her eyes.

'It's me. Rod Chi. Up here, Mrs Roberts!'

'Why Rodney,' she stopped her sweeping and walked
across the grass to stand beneath the window. 'You've
come across to be with us. How nice. Is your sister—?'

'Yes, yes, and maybe my mum!'

'That's lovely to hear. The whole family…'

'Yeah, but could you do me a favour, Mrs Roberts? Could
you come up here and unlock the door? Someone, Liam
maybe, locked it by mistake last night and he's not about.'

'They're all at a very important ceremony down by the
sea. One that will bless the whole community. We're
preparing for a big celebration,' she told him leaning on the
broom, glad of the diversion.

Stop talking, oh stop talking, he willed her, but she went
on, her voice filled with pleasure.

'You came over at the right time. Tonight's a real party
here. It's a shame I have very big worries right now. Very
worrying news indeed, although the Pastor said I should let
it rest on his shoulders. And I know he'll solve it for me.

That's what is so wonderful about this man. All our worries, he shoulders all of them.'

'That's great,' he could hardly keep the impatience out of his voice, 'but could you come up here and let me out?'

'Certainly,' she said. 'You should be at work down here, I'm sure. Plenty to do, you know. And I'm not one who likes to see young people idle. It's not our way here, either.'

He waited anxiously. Heard her padding up the stairs and coming along the corridor. Then silence.

'Have you found the key, Mrs Roberts?' he asked

'Well, yes Rodney, it's in the key holder right beside the door.' He waited with bated breath. It couldn't be this easy. It wasn't!

'Mrs Roberts,' he called out, 'open the door, Mrs Roberts, or I won't get down there in time.'

'That's just it, Rodney.'

'What's just it?'

'I can't remember the key rule but I know there is one!'

'The key rule?'

'We have rules for everything here you know. And one of them is the key rule and I can't quite remember. Better check with someone.'

He heard her departing steps and sat on the bed. Five past eleven and she was going to check with someone! Another five minutes passed before she returned.

'Can't find any of the men but lucky I remembered for myself.'

'The key rule?' he asked dismayed.

'Permission of three to open a locked door. Permission of three. So lucky I didn't do anything wrong. You'll just have to wait until someone else with authority comes back. Until two more come back. Won't be long, I'm sure.'

'Mrs Roberts,' he called out, desperate now. 'Look I'm embarrassed but you'll have to open it without permission. See I need to go to the bathroom. Then you can lock the door again.'

'There are chamber pots under every bed. This Centre is a really old hotel,' and she laughed. 'We all used chamber pots in the good old days and the Pastor said to leave them there. If they were good enough for us—specially in the rooms that have to locked—' She stopped as if giving something away.

'Locked? What rooms have to be locked?' he asked.

'Better get back to my chores.'

'Mrs Roberts,' he called urgently. 'Mrs Roberts, don't go.' He wasn't sure he should do this but he was desperate. 'It's about your grandson, Vaughan.'

'Oh Vaughan,' and he heard her sigh. 'That's my worrying news, you see. He's gone. The Pastor came and broke it to me this morning. They went over last night to invite him here but he'd left the town altogether, which is such a worry for me. I'm the one responsible and I did leave without him. But the Pastor insists it was his choice not to come here and in the end it will be a better thing for our little community, if young Vaughan really didn't want to stay here with us. We can't have negativity or opposition like that.

'They're going to say special prayers for him today. They're worried about him losing his way in the desert. They've reported it to the police, of course, and there's a group out looking now. He was always so set against anything the Pastor said. I just hope—'

'He hasn't gone,' Rod told her. 'In fact, Mrs Roberts, he could be in great danger. That's why I've got to ask you to break a rule. To open the door. I just might be able to help Vaughan. He's down there at the sea, I'm certain, and they intend to harm him! Believe me! They have plans to harm him!'

He couldn't see her look of horror and the way she recoiled as if she had just realised a devil in the guise of Rodney Chi dwelt in the small storeroom, but he heard her intake of breath.

'Then it's true what the Pastor said. There must be an aura of evil growing around you to tell such a lie. Oh my God, it's true!' and her hurried frightened footsteps carried her away from him and away from the truth.

He was defeated. Well and truly. Vaughan's grandmother unwilling to do anything that might offend the Pastor, even for her own blood relation. Unwilling to consider anyone else. Unwilling to hear the truth. Where was Nona then? Where was his mother? They were to meet shortly in a few hours' time. He'd stuffed up the whole thing here, and in forty-four minutes Vaughan Roberts, the pawn of the Pastor, would be forced to make a dive that would end his life.

He paced the room, he called through the window, 'Someone, anyone, come up here and let me out!' But he heard only the definite strokes of the broom beating away the dirt and dust on the tiles out front and then someone singing in the kitchen. Shit! He sank down on the floor. Fifteen minutes to twelve.

Then an unfamiliar sound, a dragging sound, as if

someone were having difficulty walking. Someone who mounted the stairs slowly, slowly. An old man or woman who'd heard him? Who out of pity or some shred of wisdom was coming his way? He heard the shuffling noise along the corridor coming nearer and nearer. He heard the someone stop right at his door. Merciful God! He crossed himself, filled with renewed hope.

'Hey Chi!' a hoarse voice came through the keyhole, a young voice, one he recognised, despite its raspy tone.

'Sandy, oh mate!'

'Yeah!'

'You okay, Sandy?'

'Yeah. No. Ankle's broken.'

'Shit!'

'Yeah, can't walk far.'

'You got a crutch?'

'No, he won't let me, not yet. But I'll be getting one, soon.'

'Open the door, mate.'

'I like it here okay, you know.'

'Sure!' Rod said. Still got his humour the old Sandy, but then he heard the words repeated and something warned him things had gone amiss with Sandy, big time!

'I like it a lot,' Sandy said again. 'Took time but you know I've changed a lot and I like it. Except for my foot, I like it! Came to tell you that. Heard you calling.'

'Sure thing, Sandy. I can understand that.'

Sweet Jesus, the key was turning in the lock.

When the door opened Sandy was standing gripping the door jamb for support, his bound foot held above the ground. The boy was pale and was almost unrecognisable for his face was battered and bruised. But he was smiling. Smiling!

'My God, what have they done to you?'

'Took a fall,' he said.

'Or two or three,' Rod commented. Pastor's handiwork again, he guessed.

'I like it here okay, you know. I like it now,' the boy began again.

'Sure mate,' Rod glanced down at his watch. It was ten minutes to twelve.

'Sandy, I gotta go. But can you meet me at Madshark this afternoon? Sandy?'

Sandy was shaking his head. 'Couldn't do that. No way.' And he hung his head. 'I like it here,' he recited, 'yes, I like it a lot now! Came to tell you that but I should lock the door again. See there's a rule of three. Don't want to break any more rules. Not ever,' and he laughed. Rod knew Sandy would be a pushover.

'You look after that foot.' Rod touched Sandy's arm in sympathy but the boy withdrew fearfully.

'Got to lock up, mate! You know that I like it here now. I said that didn't I? I really like the Master. We have an understanding.'

Rod sprang past Sandy, giving him a light push that made the lad fall back, powerless against him. And then he was down the stairs two, three at a time. When he swept by Mrs Roberts she called out ineffectually, 'You shouldn't go down there. It's only for the Cherished—' But already he was speeding over the jaggedy surface, past the stonehenged boulders and down the track that led to the rock shelf where they'd all be in readiness!

Plunge Hole and on through the Golden Gate and into the Victory Pool. But what then? If he made it, which was clearly impossible with the tide, he'd have to face them at the other end. The spears or something else? It was a hopeless cause all round. Should he even try?

The chanting died away. He looked around. Maybe he would just let them finish him off here and now.

'The holy wreath, Liam,' the Pastor called. 'Who will volunteer to place the holy wreath?'

Vaughan saw the Pastor raise the familiar circlet. And then there was a commotion, the sound of someone pounding over the rocks. The police, he thought hopefully. Oh please God, let it be the police come to stop this madness! The boys with the spears turned in disarray for a moment. Then Vaughan saw someone familiar and dear. He watched as Rod leapt forward and a few of the men grabbed at him. But Rod struggled towards the place where the Pastor stood, dragging the men with him. He hadn't even looked Vaughan's way. And Rod was yelling out, 'No, let me!' And he was reaching for the circlet. 'Master, please, let me!'

'Release him!' the Pastor said.

Vaughan was incredulous as Rod threw himself down at the Pastor's feet and begged, 'Please Master, you've allowed me to be close to you. Please let me be the Chosen One.'

'You are not yet one of the Inner Circle.'

'This can be my test of faith, surely.'

Vaughan swallowed back tears. The only person he could call his friend in this godforsaken hole had joined them. The only friend, who a night ago was trying to help him out of here, was now choosing to crown him for what could only be his death swim.

The Pastor raised his eyes skywards as if seeking wisdom and then he looked down at Rod.

'Let him be our brother,' he said. And the others nodded in agreement. Slowly Rod took the circlet from the Pastor's outstretched hand.

A wave of anger was replaced by a wave of hope as the burly figure, wreath in hand, approached. Surely Rod would do something—push them all away, make some heroic movie-type action that would get them out of here. Then a wave of despair washed over Vaughan as Rod raised the crown Nona's deft hands had made, without making eye contact with him at all.

'Birth, destruction and renewal!' Rod yelled, mad as they, looking back over his shoulder and egging them on. The chant grew fiercer and louder again. *'Birth destruction and renewal.'* Rod leant towards him, a crazy look in his eye. 'In the Cathedral...air for you. Look for it. Go!' he hissed.

The chanting died down and the Pastor moved forward again. 'Go with our blessing to the Palace of Coral Kings and the Salts of Excellence to heal the rift of the Spirit Waters. For all shall at last be made peaceful and good.'

There was a strange cry and Vaughan looked round. It was Liam, white-faced, calling out as if to stop him. But the Pastor moved in quickly, wrapping strong arms around the boy's shuddering body.

'Chant the chant,' he heard him say and then Liam's faltering voice joining the Pastor's, *'Birth, destruction and renewal.'* The words were taken up once again in a chorus of frenzy. And Rod's voice seemed to boom above it.

The Pastor gave the signal and the butcher urged Vaughan forward to the lip of the pool. No need for force. He was already taking in the salt air, puffing out his chest with desperate hope, till he must have looked almost the size of Rod. Though he concentrated on this inhalation his eyes seemed to take in the whole world at that moment. To the left, the rim of the beach and far off craggy mountains of rock. To the right, the cave entrance, undistinguished, a blackish mouth at high tide. And to the far right the Pastor presiding over Liam. And though he didn't turn around he knew, could sense the tight ring of boys brandishing their spears right behind him.

Vaughan dived deep, making the cave entrance with ease, the straggly weed caressing his body as he passed inside. He moved forward through the Devil's Gullet, making good time, he was sure, to the Shark Pool. You could feel the gullet open out. Rod said it was the shape of a shark but who could really tell in the dark.

'It'll get real thin again before the Cathedral. Don't even think of releasing any air until you reach the Waist,' he heard Rod's instructions. It seemed aeons ago. Well, he'd come this far before and his young strong arms took him forward now at such speed he passed the Waist without any desire to expel air.

'Don't be afraid of the dark, use the walls to help pull you through the Narrows.' This was unfamiliar territory and he felt the first impulse to release some breath. 'Slow as, with the air,' Rod had said, 'just a little at a time. Slow as, mate.'

Cautiously, slowly, his head quite clear, his strong lungs filled with the effort, Vaughan breathed out the first bit of precious air. Bubbles flew around him and he was filled with a ridiculous, quite ridiculous hope. He was in control for the moment. There, already the blessing of light up ahead and it had been so easy. He couldn't believe it because the light meant he had reached the Cathedral, and he had let just a little air out, by no means all. It was further than he thought but he'd done better than he thought.

He eased out a little more air, and a little more, and then the tunnel opened out dramatically. Volcanic flanges created curtains of stone that revealed the dome-shaped cavern behind them, brilliant with light and little tropical fish. Vaughan was beginning to feel the need to expel more of his air. A little more, and a little more and he held back the last of it. His eyes searched desperately. 'You go to the surface and low tide there's a pocket where you can breathe. The air's that sweet, mate. Nothing in the world as sweet as when you suck in that air there.'

But this was high tide. There was no place to gulp sweet air necessary for the second part of this journey. None that he could find. Yet Rod had mouthed the words which had given him hope and strength. 'In the Cathedral. Air for you. Look for it!'

His arms swung round wildly. He should leave the place and try to make the second part of the swim, impossible now for most of the air was gone. A tearing pain and a great expulsion of air left his lungs all but empty. He couldn't make it. There was the desire to inhale and inhale, his lungs seemed to be bursting with the need. He would die down here as the Pastor wanted. Couldn't make the Radiant Way now, the Golden Gate or the Victory Pool. Could not.

But his raging, flailing hands hit smooth steel and then he saw the air tank, wedged tight against the ceiling behind a rock curtain, well within his reach. His hand fumbled over the mouth piece but he knew, he knew he could last the distance now. He wouldn't inhale for a few moments…no! He'd take the time, time, time, to fit the mouth piece correctly, click the air flow on, though he thought he'd just about burst with the effort to do so. He couldn't use the exhalation method to clear the regulator of water. He had no breath left for that. But his strong young hands found the purge button. His tongue eagerly blocked the mouthpiece, exactly as in the Padi lessons Rod had given him, and he pushed the button to release air from the tank. He cleared the regulator so that yes, oh yes, he could take in that air, he could breathe. Breathe at last!

'Rodney bloody beauty!' The gush of sweet air down his throat replenished his flaccid, aching lungs. Breath of life! His heart was racing with new hope. He was hungry for that air and he gulped deep, deep draughts of it. But he should try to calm his breathing style right now! He remembered the rule most impressed on him by his tireless, relentless instructor: you never, never hold your breath with compressed air in your lungs. So he wouldn't stop breathing, just slow it down. 'Slow as!' Every detail of every lesson seemed to flood back as the oxygen replenished his young body. Yes, it was as sweet as Rod had said. The sweetest!

He had twenty good minutes of oxygen, he knew that. And somebody, that underwater angel, had left a mask for him as well. This would make the wait in his underwater cavern more bearable. Though he would not be able to empty the mask of water entirely, he could see exactly where he was. He slipped the mask on, remembering the lessons again. He held the top of the mask hard against his forehead and began, with the luxury of lungs full of air, exhaling through his nose. Gradually the cave became clearer and clearer as the water dispersed and he could see through the mask. His heart stopped racing, his breathing became quite regular.

Vaughan, hand to the ceiling to steady himself, prayed in his watery cathedral—not for his salvation for he knew he'd been saved—but a prayer of thanks, crossing himself and luxuriating in the ability to do so. The light at the top of the cave bathed the place in green, even the multitude of yellow and black striped fish passing by unconcernedly had a greenish glow. He was among them now, the little schools of bright-coloured fish, alive and one of them! A fish himself.

There was the rest of the swim to make without the tank but he was more than halfway, Rod had said, once in the Cathedral. Vaughan knew he could do it. He'd proved he could do it.

Now he could make plans. He'd wait here in the Cathedral for as long as he dared. They would more than likely leave, come back down at low tide for him, several hours away. Sending someone in, the best swimmer, probably Dyson, to bring him out of there. They'd discover the poor foolish boy had drowned. Alert the Compound and the authorities, break the sad news to his grandmother, to Younger than Springtime or whatever they called her in there. But later, secretly, he imagined the Inner Circle would hold a dance of victory and the ceremony of Liam's release. Well, he could wait for that! They could all wait forever and a day! He was no bloody sacrificial lamb. Sacrificial fish, he thought.

It was difficult to judge the time. Snatches of familiar songs went through his head, as they so often did. He concentrated on remembering. *What'll I do/ when you/ are far away/ and I am blue/ what'll I do?* Concentrating on the words and not on his absent parents. He watched fish come and go, he explored the intricacies of the cavern with its bunches of weed and its vaulted rock walls. Then he realised he was beginning to feel quite chilly. Rod had told him that water always conducts heat away from the body much faster than air, despite the warm tropical tides here. He was beginning to shiver. He should go on. He could see the Plunge Hole—the way out—so small no air tank could fit through.

But he wouldn't be fazed by that thought because he could, and he would, get there. He was so close now. He'd make it through the Golden Gate and once he'd reached the Victory Pool he'd go over the edge into the ocean and swim around to Madshark Cove as fast as he could. Hide there in the sandhills until night and take a different track to get away. He felt a surge of triumph even before he plucked the precious airtube from his mouth.

Then he was through the Plunge Hole, grazing one shoulder in the effort, unaware of a stream of blood following. The Radiant Way was just that and he released a chain of silver bubbles that sped their way to a meniscius of spun gold.

Vaughan burst through the wavering surface of the Victory Pool, despite his plan to ascend with caution, sucking in air hungrily. Victorious! Then he saw a face. There'd be others behind it and spears...But it was Nona Chi, and no one else in sight. She had his shirt in her hand.

'Well done, Vaughan! Thank God you're okay!' and she smiled at him. 'I came back here after they went...'

'I'm going round to Madshark,' he told her, clearing his eyes of water, trying to quell a rush of strangling emotion.

'No, you'd better not. The current's strong right now and they're fishing over there. Go over the hills, to the Furrows.'

Vaughan hauled himself out of the pool, shivering in the sun, his skin spongy, his mind water-logged.

'Don't go back in the water. That's where they'll look! And you're way too cold. I know what I'm talking about.' She seemed older, more self-possessed than he remembered her.

'I don't know.' His hands began to shake now and he had an urge to cry which he suppressed with an angry retort. 'Anyway, why should I do what you say? How do I know if I should trust you?'

'I'm here, aren't I? And how do you think the air tank got there?'

He looked into her eyes and he knew it was true, that this young girl had done the lonely, difficult dive for him. Then he looked around at this seaside world, suddenly glad to be here, glad to be alive, glad she was there beside him.

They crouched together in an encircling arm of warm dark rock. He couldn't speak for a few moments and she let him gather himself. At his feet Vaughan saw festering seaweed, some faded periwinkles, the bubbling slime of a sea pond dying in the sun.

Life, he thought unaccountably as he looked up at her.

'Rod was baled up by the Pastor. But we have code words for scuba diving see. He knew I could get the tank from the Lonely Place and get it inside the Cathedral, but he had to let *you* know. That was the worst bit. Thank God they let him in at the last moment.'

'You made the dive for me?' He looked at her slight form, wondering how she'd managed to take even the small air tank through that difficult passageway. It had taken him all summer to feel he could attempt it and even then he'd hung back for fear.

'Made it dozens of time. Liam taught me. Secretly of course. First he wouldn't let me anywhere near the place. Remember the first time I met you? I was so worried you'd tell? But then, once he'd told me all about Benny, he said he was keen for me to learn how to do it. I've always been a good swimmer and I did it pretty easily. Those boys think they're so macho!' she said scornfully. Then her tone changed. 'You know that Benny was Liam's little brother?' Vaughan nodded. He'd heard that name all too often.

'They were very close. Unusually close you could say. Liam teased Benny, just like big brothers do, and they had a fight. On that day little Benny took a friend to watch and tried to make amends, doing the dive to impress Liam. The friend screamed the town down, looking for Liam when Benny didn't surface. It was Liam who found him dead, drowned in the Cathedral, and fetched him out. Liam's felt guilty, forever. People say it changed him big time. He dropped out of school quick smart. They say he drank a lot, too.'

'I didn't know all that,' Vaughan said, frowning and picturing a drowned boy down there with a mouth full of blood.

He stood up a moment, his eyes searching the horizon. Nona must have felt his tension.

'Look, take my purple shirt, it'll help get you through. And I'll wear this one.' Unselfconsciously she tore off the blouse she was wearing and handed it to him, dabbing his blood wet shoulder before putting on his shirt. She even laughed, 'They'll think you're one of us!'

Her tenderness was disarming. He wanted to say something but could find no words.

'Go over the headland by rock and then up the Furrows. You could wait there till evening, less likely to be seen then.'

'Are you coming?'

'I've told Mum and Rod I'll meet them at Madshark. We'll head for Cat Harbour—if Rod's doing what he said he would about the car—and come back here with the police.'

'What...and arrest them all for praying?' Vaughan said as he pulled on the thin purple fabric.

'No, for something much more serious.' She touched his arm and a sympathy seemed to flow between them. He looked away.

Though he was warming up fast now, he had given an involuntary shudder at her words. It didn't bear thinking about the fact that he could be bobbing around in the Cathedral right now, breathless, moving with the ebb and flow of the water. Lifeless, like the boy in the dream.

It was at this moment Vaughan realised something about the drowned face that startled him. The boy in his strange, recurring dream had not been Benny at all! The face wasn't Benny's or Liam's. The one he'd pictured so often, yet whose features remained blurry, suddenly came into sharp focus. It was him! The boy who'd drowned down there in his dreams was him. For sure! Well, he hadn't! He wouldn't! The Pastor would be eternally disappointed.

'In your dreams,' he said out loud, astonished but also relieved, as if the dream cycle which had haunted him was all over and done with.

'What?' Nona frowned at him. 'What about your dreams?'

'A premonition—has to be. A nightmare I've been having ever since I came here. Doesn't matter.' Then he asked sharply, shaking the image away forever, 'What's Rod doing?'

'He knows a way out.'

'You should go, soon as you can.'

She shook her head. 'I've got to see Liam one last time.'

'But why?' He thought of the shuddering, useless youth, truly the Pastor's pawn now.

'Liam's kind of in love with the Pastor. Father figure I reckon. I don't know why but he's got no will of his own any more. The Pastor's talking Eternal Peace too much for my liking. And Liam started talking suicide last night. Look, I feel nothing but pity for Liam any more, it's all so terrible. He's changed so much. But I just can't leave him without trying one more time. Sometimes, you know, sometimes, even now, he listens to me.' Her eyes seemed full of pain and Vaughan's heart went out to her.

'But the others? All the people here in the Compound.

Why haven't some of them worked things out for themselves?'

'I don't know. Seems like the Pastor's lifted them out of
desperation. Out of themselves in some weird way. The
Compound's become the centre of the universe to them.
And he's all-powerful there. He's become, well, I guess he's
become their god!'

He didn't quite know why he dared but without thinking Vaughan reached towards Nona and kissed her. Perhaps
it was to do with the bravery of this quicksilver girl. Perhaps
he thought she looked beautiful and earnest with the afternoon sun in her dark curly hair. Perhaps it was the only way
he knew to thank her. It was not a brotherly kiss and she
didn't attempt to stop him. He saw she had tears in her
eyes as she turned away from him.

'You better get going!' she told him.

He thought the salt he tasted on his lips must be partly
hers and that pleased him immensely as he made his way
towards the Furrows.

NINETEEN

As he clambered over the rocks a boat came in. The men waved, obviously mistaking him for someone from the Compound, and he waved back. Vaughan increased his pace, slipping and sliding until he got round the headland. He worked his way up the tussocky sandhills towards the most remote of them.

The Furrows, so called because they were like great creases in a worried forehead, were not sandhills anyone would choose to visit. Some years ago a group of little kids had disappeared in the sand, playing and digging there. His grandmother had told him stories—young, sobbing voices heard on the wind from time to time. Kids in the town who showed any interest in the place were told there was quicksand here. Might as well be, Vaughan thought, sliding along the silky edges of sand that crumbled and slipped away despite his careful footfalls.

He'd wait here until dark. He'd be too easily seen on the crests of those white hills. He found a comfortable enough place between two low sandhills, where the earth was harder and some driftwood did as a kind of pillow and he settled down. But an annoying breeze sent particles flying into his eyes, his ears and his nose and he pulled Nona's shirt up over his face. He thought of her then—her bright brown eyes and slender athletic figure, her creamy brown skin. She'd risked everything to help him. *Nona*. Aboriginal for girl. *Nona*. There was no song he could think of that his father had once strummed but there was something, dredged up from schooldays back east, about that familiar-sounding name.

An afternoon looking at Aboriginal poetry in the library and Noah Markham—yes, he even remembered the class clown's name—had made everyone laugh. At the teacher's request to memorise six lines of an Aboriginal poem, Noah had chosen the poem 'Nona' by the poet Oodgeroo of the tribe of Noonuccal because it mentioned the nakedness of Nona, 'the lithe and lovely'. The kids had responded as Noah expected, with guffaws of laughter. But the teacher had responded, too. The class had to write out Oodgeroo's name fifty times before going to recess and Noah Markham had to write it five hundred times. Well, Vaughan had remembered Oodgeroo of the tribe Noonuccal for those fifty times he'd penned her name! He'd always liked the sound of it. And a fragment of her poem about a girl called Nona.

Where was Nona now? he wondered. And would she, would they get through? All the effort of his survival, the frightening incarceration as he'd waited and wondered, flooded back and he was exhausted by it. There was so far to go to Cat Harbour. If he were tribal Aboriginal he'd be quite at home here in the hills. He'd find food and water and make the trek north with ease, he thought. Well, he wasn't, but he was still determined to make it somehow. He should rest for the moment and then go hell for leather in the cool and the dark, keeping in the shadows of the hills this time.

When he woke up and pulled the thin material away from his face, there was a vast, starry sky above him, so clear he lay for full moments searching and finding, a game he'd played with his mother, centuries ago, it seemed. There was the Southern Cross and the Saucepan, yes, and the powdery fineness of the Milky Way. His mother had told him as a young child that you could swim in that milky river of stars. 'Starry, starry night,' he sang in his head along with his mother, his father's guitar softly in the background.

'If only you could see me now!' He almost said it out loud but he was jumpy and he didn't know where the Compound people hung out, how far they'd go to find him. They'd have discovered, or at least *not* discovered, his dead body by now. They'd figure the current had sucked him back out and over the rocks maybe. Or they'd think he'd made a miraculous escape and go searching for him by sea and by land. Hunt him out and…it didn't bear thinking about right now.

As his eyes searched the familiar sky, naming the stars, there was the sudden weight of his absent parents to contend with again. The stars, so stridently clear, seemed to pulse and flicker at him, their frosty glitter cruel and mocking now. He felt so alone here.

It was still quite incredible to Vaughan to think people in a community close by had tried to *kill him* only hours before. Kill him! And his own grandmother had no idea of the kind of people who were part and parcel of her new found home, though she was obviously prepared to live with them quite happily. Or maybe she did have an idea and silently approved it! No, he couldn't really believe that of the puffing, complaining, even the hypnotised January—not that!

But it didn't change the fact that a dozen or more boys and men, seemingly normal people, under the influence of such a compelling, demanding, all-promising leader, had become common killers almost overnight. They had forced him to make a swim knowing the impossibility of his survival, and no one among them had lifted a finger to help him. In the end it had been Rod and Nona. Thank God for Rod and Nona! But the others had gone along with the Pastor willingly, taken part in a monstrous act. Despite the warmth of the night Vaughan's teeth began chattering at the realisation, the enormity of it.

Why think of this now? Why waste time on those insects? Why not get going! But their expressionless faces, those boys, those men in the grim line up, appeared before him and he heard the chanting begin and he felt incapable of anything, certainly of any more plans. Vaughan was exhausted, despite his nap, and a shuddering desolation seemed to overwhelm him.

Starry, starry night…Now he had a sudden image of his parents on another starlit beach, an image so vivid and so painful he cried out in anguish, mindless of the marauding forces around him. The pain of a longing that was almost unbearable made him rise to his feet.

'Starry, starry night, Dad!' he called out to the dark. 'Starry bloody night, Mum,' he yelled at the sky. And then to ease the awful hammering, panicky feeling he began walking in circles that got faster and wilder as he measured his aloneness. 'Starry starry night,' he whispered over and over trying to blot out the terrifying incantation back there. *Birth, destruction and renewal!* He would never, ever be able to forget. The cold, killer eyes of the Pastor making them repeat it. Making Liam, all of them, do it. And the blank indifferent stares the others were able to maintain through his agony and fear. Pitiless stares.

'Starry, starry, starry, starry,' he chanted quicker and quicker, louder and louder but there was the dark cave entrance with its flailing seaweed arms rising up and the cold dark swim he'd made in blind desperation as the others up top had rejoiced. 'To hell with you!' he yelled down the Furrows, not caring if he were inviting disaster. 'To hell with the lot of you!' And then he stopped in his tracks and great heaving sobs seemed to be wrung out of a deep part of his chest where the pain burrowed and clutched at him.

He fell back on the sand and the stars were blurry and cold through his tears. He cried bitterly because he felt, through no fault of his own, he had been cast out into the wilderness. He'd come through the dark, terrifying tunnel with his all his hope and his life force contained in his controlling breath. He'd been able to snatch the gift of life that Nona had left him by way of the air tank, and then once more make a terrifying dive, and get through! He'd been helped on his way by the gutsy Nona, waiting and risking everything to help him. But what was going to now happen to him now? And why was he left alone like this to try to find his own way?

What was worse was the realisation that whether he made it or not tonight, his parents did not know about his predicament. And they didn't care despite their barrage of guilty letters which had been followed by a long silence. They had left him to his fate. No, they'd *abandoned* him to his fate. They were ignorant of what was going on and liked it that way. Ignorant of whether he'd had to face death and madness here, or cruelty and despair. Well, stuff them and their endless repertoire of songs, their empty promises. He'd not think of them or their songs ever again!

And yet the maddening lyrics ran on in his head long after he was silent and left shuddering with a grief that recognised them as dead to him. There was a sudden image of his father's shoulder, the warmth and breadth of it where his own childish head had rested close against it. He couldn't stop the play of memory though it brought tears to his eyes again. The three of them sitting on the sand—their one and only beach holiday at Seal Rocks so long ago. They'd left the caravan park simmering in the afternoon sun and swum in the ice green waves. They'd larked on the sand, his father boyish, and unusually active, unusually patient with him, his mother tolerant and smiling. They'd made a campfire on the beach and as the darkness fell Vaughan had felt, aware of their closeness to each other and to him, that this was one of the happiest days of his life. Even in his childish, vague knowledge that they were 'in the eye of the storm' of his parents' unpredictable relationship, he enjoyed the harmony of that evening together. Believed that time had stood still for them to be happy in...

'Starry, starry night,' his father had crooned by the camp-fire light looking deep into his wife's eyes. And Vaughan had noticed they held hands. Later, as he was falling asleep against his father's shoulder, he fought off the tiredness because he wanted to savour the moment. His father's voice and then her light one joining his. The full play of that memory somehow calmed his racing heart. He stopped hating them altogether and the overwhelming self pity that had crippled him moments ago began to recede.

'Well, bugger them and the dreams that took them the hell out of here,' he thought. 'I've got to get on the best way I can.' He'd not sit here railing against the stars or his parents. What was the use? He'd push on. That's what he'd do.

He should wait until the dead of night to leave the Furrows. Dead! he was able to smile as he thought of the word. He should have been dead, would have been, if it hadn't been for a brother and sister. No. No more waiting. It was dark enough now. He'd make for Five Mile and maybe he'd find them. A day's walk to get anywhere away from this hell-hole. He was already quite thirsty and regretted not spending a little time looking for a container as Rod had told him to the day before. But he'd been so eager to leave the Settlement far behind while the going was good. He'd try to find a tin, something to collect the dew when he got near the road. If there was nothing, he knew the strange desert flowers that bloomed in some of the foothills were convenient receptacles. Rod had shown him once how you could extract water from them. Already his mind was racing ahead to Five Mile, his hopes rising that the Chi family would be there waiting. He thought of Nona's enthusiasm, reflecting one of Rod's favourite phrases. 'You'll make it if you go now—piece of cake!'

He stood and brushed his sandy hair back and wiped his eyes clear. No more whimpering. The starry, starry night would help him get through the Furrrows and go on beside the highway. Piece of cake for sure!

It was heavy going through the soft sand but he went on doggedly, guided by the stars. Within an hour Vaughan noted that the character of the landscape was changing and he felt the earth underfoot harden. He knew, though he could not see clearly in the moonlight, that it had changed colour, dramatically reddened and coarsened as he neared the highway. He walked on, stepping it out on the red earth, knowing that not long after first light there'd be a sun that burned through the light cotton of Nona's shirt, pinching his shoulders and blazing down on his head unmercifully.

He'd be slowed down by thirst, too, for though he'd found the strange desert blooms, there was nothing to carry water in. He'd supped from several of them and then plucked one fleshy receptacle with its tiny supplement of water to carry with him. A bit of a joke for there was a mere mouthful but it was comforting somehow. Maybe he'd find others.

He saw the ramshackle remains of the garage that constituted Five Mile probably a kilometre before he arrived. Its corrugated water tanks and its corrugated roof shone in the moonlight, as did the rusting petrol bowsers out front.

The windows, miraculously intact in the body of the building, glinted. He skirted the place first of all, aware he might
be ambushed. But as the minutes ticked by and nothing
stirred within or without, Vaughan made his approach. He
was all too aware that there was no car parked there. The
Chi's were not here, nobody else either.

His thirst drove him inside the building and he was
rewarded for the tap at the cobwebbed sink hissed and spat
when he turned it on, first rusty and then clearer water.
Drinkable water for sure. After he'd taken his fill, he found
a place in the corner where he could take up a position to
view the road. It would be easy to slip away into the dark
should anyone approach. In this way he wouldn't miss the
Chi's car but could avoid anyone else. If they didn't come
in the next few hours he'd go on, with water this time for
he'd found a few rusted tins in a pile of rubbish. He sat
sleepily through another hour, his hope dying as minutes
ticked by. He'd have to move on by himself.

It wasn't the lights of the car that caught his attention so
much as the sound of the motor, a distant throbbing echo-
ing across the wastelands at last.

He was out the back of the building and in hiding well
before the car pulled up. He saw figures jump out of the
car, one a woman, one a youth and one a girl.

'Hey, Vaughan! You there, Vaughan?' he heard the voice
call through the night. There was no need to wonder
whether it was friend or foe.

'Here!' he called and the relief he felt made it impossible
to say another word until he'd joined them. Nona jumped
at him in joy and hugged him fiercely, then Rod and Mrs
Chi followed suit.

'Hurry and get in,' Rhonda Chi told them, 'we shouldn't delay!'

'Mum would've had you leap in the backdoor as we sped by if she could,' Nona joked. 'She's that jumpy.' When Vaughan climbed in beside Nona she took his hand and pressed it in her own warm one.

'They'll know in the morning we've gone and they'll send someone looking.' Rhonda Chi clashed the gears as the car took off.

'We had a hell of a time getting out of there,' Rod began explaining, 'that's why we're so late. We thought we'd be waiting for you!' Then Rhonda Chi took over and told Vaughan admiringly of the way Rod had fixed the car.

'Had to break into the garage, desperate for the tyres but couldn't get us any petrol. There wasn't any to be had! What a panic. Then Rod remembered a storehouse of petrol at the Compound and he pinched it from right under their noses. It took him hours and we were all terrified—but inspired too—because we knew you'd come through. Nona told us all about that.' She turned to smile at Vaughan briefly. 'It was the best news of all!'

It appeared that Vaughan's 'body' had not been fetched yet from the Cathedral so there was no alarm at all. The massive preparations for feasting and celebration that had made it all the easier for the Chi's to escape were well underway. Rod had delayed Rhonda and Nona by looking for Sandy but he was nowhere to be found.

'More about all of that later, mate. What about you?' he asked, sensing Vaughan's exhaustion.

'Nothing much to tell,' Vaughan said, 'except tramp bloody tramp across the sand!'

They all laughed but Vaughan had to shove away thoughts of what had gone before. He was safe now. Almost.

'It's about five hours to Cat Harbour and not much between here and there,' Rhonda Chi told him. 'A two-bit township on the way but I wouldn't risk stopping there. We'll push on through the night.'

'Can't you just see their faces when they find the Cathedral empty?' Rod asked.

There was hysterical laughter from all the occupants of the car but Vaughan was close to tears again and Rhonda must have guessed.

'They'll be up for an attempted murder charge that lot!' she snapped. 'Soon as we get to Cat Harbour.'

The car raced across the red earth and began the climb up the first of the hills, formations too low to be called mountains. At the summit something made Vaughan turn round, to look back at land he felt they'd overcome, land he'd never see again. It had been alien territory to him with its brooding volcanic formations. Far away, over towards the coast and clearly at the Settlement there was a sudden burst of flames that shot up into the sky.

'God, the place's going up like a bomb!' he yelled and his alarm brought the car to a halt. They all jumped out to view intermittent explosions on the horizon.

'Settlement's going up in flames, Mum,' Nona burst out, 'Oh Liam! Mum! Poor Liam!'

'Calm down.' Rhonda Chi caught hold of Nona's hand. 'I reckon it's the empty houses going up, street by street. There's not a family left in the town now. Bet you anything you like the Compound'll stand intact. The Pastor values his own skin too much to do anything like that. Liam'll be fine, Nona.'

'I should go back there,' Nona flashed. 'I shouldn't have left. We should try to get him out.'

'We can't,' her mother replied. 'Not now, Nona, and you know that.'

'But why should the Pastor want to do that?' Vaughan asked, thinking of his grandmother and her ramshackle house.'Why burn down the town?'

'With all the houses and the shops gone, there's no going back for anyone who might change their mind now, is there? Part of the master plan,' Rod said.

'I think you're right, Rod,' Rhonda Chi was trying to judge things as another burst of flame marked the sky. 'It seems all to the east of the town, towards Madshark.' She turned back to the car. 'He's a raving madman. And now some of them'll see it! Mad!'

Rhonda gave Nona another hug before hurrying them all back into the car. 'Try not to worry, Nona, love. I'm sure Rod's right. Liam will be fine and we'll get him and the other boys out of there. Police'll be there tomorrow as long as we keep on course. Keep going now.'

'I asked him, I begged him to come!' she burst out. 'He almost did but then…'

'You told Liam we were going! Nona, how could you? You know bloody well he'll spill the beans to the Pastor.' Rod was indignant. 'You've just gone and endangered the lot of us, you know that!'

'He said he wouldn't say a thing,' she answered stubbornly. 'He even said at one stage that he was sick about what happened at Devil's Gullet and that he might come with us. I didn't tell him about the tank though, I didn't tell him any of that.'

'I should think not!' her brother blazed.

'No one's followed us, Rod,' Rhonda intervened. 'No one's followed yet and by the time they do, we'll be out of this. So leave her alone. What's done is done back there, as far as we're concerned.'

They drove on for minutes through a bristling silence and then Rhonda added, 'And Vaughan's been through a terrible ordeal already. He doesn't need to hear us fighting right now.'

'We're not fighting,' Rod began, 'it's just I can't believe she'd be so—so dumb about Liam!'

'Don't use words like that,' Nona flashed, 'I'm *sorry* for Liam. I think I'm the only one who really understands him. And God knows he needs someone!'

'He's got the Pastor!' Rod said and that silenced her.

'You must be exhausted. Why don't you have a sleep, Vaughan?' Rhonda Chi had caught sight of Vaughan's anxious, tired face in the rear vision mirror.

'I'm fine,' he said. As the car shot forward they saw the hint of the small settlement ahead and Rhonda tensed in the driver's seat. 'A few folk here are with the Pastor so we're going through this place top pace. Okay?'

The town was in darkness, Only a night owl stirred, bursting out of one of three straggly trees that marked some kind of taming of the hot, bare earth at the edge of this excuse for a town. No one spoke as they skimmed through there, almost as if the sleeping townspeople might be roused if they did. As they pulled away and entered more low hills, Rod and his mother began to talk in quiet tones.

'You know why he wanted Liam with him so badly?' Rod was saying. 'Like Sandy said, he gets all the youth of the town with Liam. And their families.'

'Exactly what I've been saying,' his mother agreed. 'Not to mention the young men from the Nooan homes—perfect for the kind of fortress he's obviously trying to build up.'

'I think they've all gone over,' Rod said.

'They're young and they're strong and they're already institutionalised and they're looking for family. The Pastor provides that. Liam brings them to him on a platter. No wonder he's planning to "ordain" Liam as soon as he can.

'And you know what I've been thinking?' Rhonda went on in low tones, 'his ritual dive, this sacrifice, actually binds them in fear in the end. All those young men have taken part in a murder—whatever he wants to call it! And he would have used it shamelessly to control that Inner Circle you were telling me about. Method in his madness for sure.'

'What I can't work out is why Liam is so—' Rod's voice died away a moment and then he continued. 'I s'pose I can, though. He was already so cut up about his brother for one thing. It made him off balance.'

'I'm glad you said it, Rod,' Rhonda Chi said quietly. 'That was my objection when I found out about Nona and Liam. It seems to me Liam was always troubled, always searching for something. Something his aunt couldn't give him, or you or Nona for that matter.

'You know, I couldn't find anything on that man but I've read about similar cults being built up just the way he's doing it, with total dependency. I suspect that he's not really on about living happily ever after either. In a few years, maybe a few months, he'll begin promising them things in another life, where all is perfect. Of course if they're prepared to go...And that's why those people back there in the Compound, whatever they think, need help!' she said, emphatic again.

'Like a bad dream now we're out of it!' Rod said.

'The thing is *they* are not!'

There was silence for a while and then they began discussing plans for Cat Harbour.

At first Vaughan strained to listen to their conversation over the thrum of the motor, but then he found his head lolling back against the seat. It seemed such a luxury to have a parent who was in control, helping plan ahead for them. For a moment he might have felt jealousy stirring but he was too tired, even for that. Nona didn't speak again, just took his hand in hers. He noted when he glanced at her in a flash of moonlight that the coral piece, the thing similar to the one his grandmother had worn, was gone from round her neck. He didn't know why this small detail pleased him so much.

He smiled at her through the dark, wondering how she could be so forgiving to Liam. Maybe it was true that she just pitied him. He closed his eyes and saw a vault of stars, concentrated on only that, and then he was asleep.

TWENTY

Cat Harbour, a gambling town flaring with neons, could be seen kilometres before the actual township was reached by road. It was a place most people came to and left by plane or by tour bus, as there was nothing but desert on approach. But the long, hot road was nevertheless dramatic, winding through a series of broad, bald, glistening hills. As the Chi's car rolled down those hills and headed towards crass-looking signs of civilisation, to Rod nothing had seemed more beautiful.

As Rod rejoiced Vaughan woke up. 'Cat Harbour coming up folks! Cat Harbour *sans* cats!' Vaughan rubbed his eyes and was filled with vast relief, despite a dull headache, that at last they had reached safety and sanity, albeit a crazy assemblage of lit-up buildings ahead, dotting and flickering high colour announcements—of what? As they got closer he could see it was everything from food, to bed, to sex, to religion, to petrol. Nona stirred beside him, looking out the window.

'Ugly-looking town, isn't it?' Rhonda Chi said.

'Maybe it's ugly as all get out,' Rod said, 'but right now folks, Miaow Harbour beats the hell out of that rocky old Settlement. Always thought it was heavy going, from the first time I set eyes on those bloody columns everywhere.'

His voice was light with relief and Vaughan could only silently agree with him. It was good to know that Rod sensed the same oppression there that he had. It would be unchanged and unchanging, the rock-filled landscape, despite explosions and fire. Was it really possible for a place to oppress, or was it what happened there, the people of the place who created the oppression? Maybe it had a history of bloodshed that went back hundreds if not thousands of years and you just felt it or—some people did. It didn't matter now. He was feeling light-hearted too, surveying the scene here.

Vaughan thought he'd never seen anything quite like Cat Harbour. It was a bit like Las Vegas in the USA which he'd seen on the movies. But it had peculiarly Australian touches. When they reached the town itself, glimpses down side streets revealed wide high verandahs, houses up on stumps, gardens of gums and palms and spiky red fists of waratahs. It seemed incongruous that the nearest big town to the Settlement—a quiet, sleepy fishing town, or one that seemed that way—should be so brassy and vulgar, heavily into gambling and everything that went with it.

The straggly palm trees that lined the main streets were the only relief from the barrage of signs and hoardings.

'We'll find a motel first. Police station second,' Rhonda

Chi told them. Finding a motel wasn't difficult. Street after street of them, each trying by way of signage to outpromise the next.

'Golden Haven! Well, the name sounds better than most,' Rhonda announced as she pulled into an empty courtyard past The Gorgeous Golden Nugget, The Spittin' Silver Dollar and The Pink Pussycat. The Golden Haven motel was all neon frontage and behind its glaring announcement they saw a brick and fibro structure that, as Rod put it, 'had not only seen better days but better years!'

'Why don't you come inside with me, Nona?' Rhonda was aware Nona had not spoken for a couple of hours and put her arm round the girl's shoulder as they went to rouse the unwilling proprietor.

Vaughan was finding it hard to believe, as he waited on the still warm apron of concrete under rustling palms, that he was actually out of the maw, out of the reach of the treacherous Settlement. He said as much to Rod.

'Love to see his face when the cops arrive there!' Rod said.

Nona came back brandishing some keys. 'Two rooms upstairs at the end. And apparently it's a feature in this dump that they have colour television! Luxury!' She laughed, seeming okay again.

'You'll want to phone your parents straight away, I guess Vaughan,' Rhonda said as they went up the flimsy stairs together. 'They should know just what's going on. I'm phoning the police of course.'

'Yes,' he answered automatically and blushed in the darkness because he didn't care to admit he had no idea where to contact them. He couldn't say to her that his parents hadn't written in weeks, months. He couldn't say that they'd never bothered to phone though they knew full well where he was! He tried to remember the place his mother had described in her last letter. He knew what was coming.

'Where exactly are they now?' Rhonda asked.

Something with a real fancy name. It came to him in a flash and, grateful for that, he spoke confidently. 'They were staying at Chateau Marmont.'

'France?' she asked.

'Hollywood,' he told her. Might as well be the wilds of Siberia, he thought.

'Are they actors or what?' It was the first time Rod had asked anything about his parents.

'Singers,' he said, not adding, 'unsuccessful, mostly out of work singers.'

'Shit, must be good. Hollywood eh?'

'No business like show business,' he answered flatly. Yes, his mother had sung that one often enough. Mother's milk it had been, he thought grimly. He hadn't been going to think about them or their wretched repertoire and here he was with the 'song for every occasion' joke his dad cracked when he was trying, often vainly, to amuse his mother. No business like show business! There was the business of being a parent, he thought bitterly. But that obviously wasn't anywhere near as interesting.

Inside, Rhonda Chi being kind to him only made his situation seem all the worse. She fussed over the bedroom's inadequacies and the fact he'd have to share with Rod who sometimes snored. Then she insisted on making inquiries for him and got through to the operator who supplied the number and code for America, and for LA and the hotel.

'While you speak with your parents, we'll go next door to phone the police. We'll go down to the station then. It's late but I expect they'll need to see us straight away.'

Vaughan nodded.

They left him alone in the ugly, over-crowded room with its lumpy chenille-covered beds and wall of shiny orange nylon curtains. His hands trembled as he dialled the number she'd written in firm, neat figures on the pad beside the bed. They trembled because there was a chance, just a chance, if things were going well, that they'd be back there. His mother had raved about the place. Despite everything, right at this minute, he wanted to hear those familiar voices so much it was making him shake. A thread of a chance.

But a few minutes of conversation with hotel staff told him differently. 'And if you do know their whereabouts, they left a considerable account behind. In fact, it would be good to have your name and address and we could send the bill on to you!'

'I'm only bloody fifteen,' he wanted to yell at the smooth-talking American clerk, 'how could I pay their bill?' But he said, 'Sure thing, yeah, I'll fix it. Yeah, I'll send you notification,' and hung up.

He looked out the grimy venetianed window at strips of the town, visible between dark palm fronds and ribbons of light. He could hear Nona and Rod and their mother moving about in the next door room, doors banging, cupboards opening, voices. He didn't want to see them. The cosy family of three next door with their concern for each other, with their mother presiding and loving and there beside them—he didn't want to talk to them at all! He didn't want to talk to the police either and go through the whole sorry story, explain how first his parents had dumped him and then his grandmother. Everything seemed to be collapsing round him again. He put his head down. It was throbbing now and there was no easing that pain or the other pain that was to do with them. Nona's laughter rang out from next door. He wanted out of here now...

Vaughan walked out of the room leaving the door wide open, down the stairs into the gaudily punctuated darkness of the town. He'd go somewhere, anywhere, away from them, he simply didn't care. The road seemed strangely dead despite the vibrating colours. He quickened his pace. Down another street until he reached what must be the main road. It was alive here, all right! Rotating, looping signs, strings of fairy lights, flashing neons in every direction. And people jostling and joking on the pavements. Crowds of them. Women in scant costumes, spruikers on the pavement yelling out their wares, music booming and calling from open doorways. Garish lights and garish faces—a kind of madlands. He paced through it all as if in a dream and at the end of the main road he didn't know why but he had an urge to run.

To run and to run, on and on through the town and through the night. Just to get away—from himself, if possible! He ran for what seemed kilometres. He ran until, sweating and panting, he came to a dead end.

■

It was on a beach that he stopped. On a concourse that had no lights, no people and only a few broken-down chairs.

He slumped into one of them, panting and heaving with exertion. He was drenched with sweat but the mad pace had not eased the dreadfulness he felt. His head was still throbbing. Pain seemed to be welling inside him even as he sat here, a huge dark bubble that wanted to burst. The waves of self pity and desperation he'd been able to wrestle with and shrug off back there in the desert were over-whelming now. He surveyed the narrow beach and the wide sea. He'd thought the Settlement was the end of the line often enough. Well, maybe he'd been wrong about that. Maybe this hole of a place, this Cat Harbour with its ridiculous name, this mean little beach, maybe this was it. He stared out at the dark water. Yeah, the end of the line for him.

They'd wanted his spirit to re-enter the sea, they'd tried to force it not twenty-four hours ago. And he'd fought, how he'd fought against them, against the water, filled with some sort of ridiculous hope. But now there was no fight, seemed no point. The dive, the escape…well, he couldn't escape himself. What a joke! His life was not worth that struggle. His life was pointless, he thought, drawn down onto the sand towards the glint of the water, so why struggle any more to prolong it? There was nowhere left to go but out there. So he'd go out there!

He stripped off his T-shirt and shorts and entered the water. Waves lapped gently. Though he was exhausted from the run, as he dived the cold jab of water enlivened him, serving to make him more determined. But as he swam out and out, he seemed to find still more energy. Further and deeper he went with unrelenting intent.

It seemed they'd won, placed some kind of curse on him

to make him long for the end like this, here in the water of Cat Harbour, the ridiculous town thrumming and gyrating behind him. Maybe his dream was prophetic after all. But he simply couldn't tire enough to let his body drift, then finally, blessedly, submerge. Whenever he stopped swimming, something, something made him tread water, fight once again to stay on top of that great lumbering, heaving sea, a tiny figure in a monstrous black saucer of night. 'Oh shit, Vaughan!' he thought over and over, 'you can't do anything right! Not even this!'

Well then he'd float and he'd just let the water take him where it would. Let Cat Harbour do it for him. He lay spreadeagled, face to the sky once more, and there was the constant reminder of the smallness of his world—the huge canopy overhead that outdid even the lights of Cat Harbour. All those paltry attempts at fake starry lighting, he thought, along all those desperate streets he'd passed by. The night sky got top billing every time.

The ocean was like a lulling cradle now. At last his head was clearing and he felt himself drifting, drifting. At last, yes, at last, he was being carried by some stray current swiftly out and out. His arms began to ache now. He was so tired. Surely it would not be long.

Absurd lashes of memory came to him as the sky undulated and stars moved round him in swirling currents. Peach trees on a small rise—someone's house—some old codger his parents had met who'd taken them in for a few months, and the smell of peaches on sticky hands. Birds feet, the uneasy, elderly red of them. Their harsh white droppings starring on the red cement of a crazed backyard path somewhere, tucked way back there. The little tabby cat he'd once briefly owned and loved for its crossed eyes. Loved to bits for that sweetly absurd face. Maybe that was at the Peach House? Yes, now he was sure of it. The cross-eyed cat and the crazy path at the Peach House. Way back.

His mother's fuzzy yellow jumper and the way she scrutinised herself so harshly with a toss of her head, at every mirror as she passed. His dad's hands on the guitar, the lashings of veins standing up as he sought and found the tune.

Then he saw big green bushes out the back of January's house. Hyd-er-angeas, she called them. 'Only plants to withstand the sand,' she'd say as she watered them with an inadequate punctured hose. January! A feeling of despair at the thought of her out there at the Compound right now. They could all go to hell! He'd soon be far, far away from everybody, far, far away from Cat Harbour. Far, far away from himself and a pathetic range of memories about what amounted to a bunch of nobodies. And then he thought of Nona. Her lustrous eyes looking into his with concern or…What? Something more perhaps? Nah—' she'd been so involved with Liam. But…her warm hand holding his in the car and the charge of electricity on that first contact, then the lulling comfort of it that followed, allowing him to fall asleep. Forget it!

He raised his head. How bloody long was this going to take? Then he saw the town lights were nearer, not further! And when he reached down, his hand actually touched sand! He had not drifted out to the horizon at all, but in and in. He was on the bloody shore! He sat in the shallows and he actually laughed, feeling like a little kid. He'd been saved for the second time and God in heaven that must mean something. He stood up and shook the water from his hair, his body feeling a bit like a shaggy dog. Hell, it was cold too!

What was he doing here? he wondered as he walked up the beach. He was grateful to be on dry land again. Grateful. How could his feelings see-saw like this over an hour, a few hours? 'I must need help,' he thought, drying himself with his shirt, dressing quickly. 'Man, I must need help!'

It didn't take long to find it. Nona met him in one of the back streets. His heart lifted when he saw her.

'Midnight swim?' she asked him, noting his damp shirt and wet hair.

'Taken a liking to swimming in the dark,' he replied. 'Do tunnels underwater pretty well, too!'

'Oh Vaughan.' He saw her sympathetic face and felt she understood something that even he didn't. 'Things are never that bad, you know.'

'Aren't they?'

'We're all here. Rod's at the top of the street now. We came looking. Mum's in the car back there, too. We were worried for you. I was really worried.'

He didn't move. He felt tears rising and was embarrassed. He looked away.

'Come home,' Nona said. The thought of the gaudy motel room almost made him smile—home! There was a long moment when he seemed undecided about what to do, what to say.

'Vaughan,' she spoke his name so softly. He looked at her and she put out her hand to him. 'You've got to come home with us,' she repeated.

He cleared his throat nervously. There were still no

words to be found. Maybe he should move on. Just move on. He faltered.

'You will come, won't you?' she wasn't about to give up. He looked at her brown hand shining enticingly in the dark, offered delicately the way someone might encourage a stray. He softened.

He took the proffered hand and pulled her towards him. And when they kissed he whispered fiercely, 'Yes, yes! I will.'

■

Rod was uneasy. He felt relieved that he had given his statement to the young policeman and was at last able to close his tired, burning eyes. Lying back in the plastic armchair, he tried to empty his mind. He dozed while his mother and sister and Vaughan with wet, rumpled hair, came and went from the uncomfortable waiting room. But his snatches of sleep were intersperesed with thoughts and dreams of the Compound. Of his friend Liam.

Rod felt separated from everyone by a sudden, inconsolable sorrow. Its force both surprised and frightened him. There was a crushing heaviness of heart and a lump in his throat as images of Liam played over, and he was glad no one asked him to speak. He knew he was being invaded by a monster of old. He recognised that feeling. He'd known it all too well when he'd found his father. All those weeks and months afterwards, he'd known it as a constant marauding companion. He'd finally been able to send it on its way, managed to hold it at bay all these years. But right now, in the harsh glare of the blue fluorescence of this room, the sly insistent guest would not be dissauded from re-entry. The black grief. Liam!

His mother—and even Vaughan—had been so busy being sympathetic to Nona that they hadn't thought of his loss. Liam had been *his* friend first, he thought. His buddy. The best mate you could ever have! They'd talked the talk of best friends. Nobody could know what that meant, what they had shared. How come the whole dreary town lit up, the air seemed brighter, things moved faster, rocks leaned over and spray foamed higher, when you were with Liam? How come? And why was there to be no more of it? And why, why had it hit him like this, right now, in such a public place?

By the sound of it, the Pastor was going to take the whole lot of them with him. Jesus, why weren't they doing something! Sending in the army? Wiping out that beast and his evil ideas. The police had said things were 'in hand' and they'd give them 'details' soon, whatever that meant. In the meantime who knew what satanic things the man was up to?

No one seemed interested in *him* right now and anyway how could he speak of the heaviness of heart, his feeling of powerlessness and his apprehension as they waited? The police wanted facts. Facts! Well it was a fact, he thought with astonishment, that he had loved Liam. He couldn't bear the thought of his friend's possible death, or his madness. His mind was full of thoughts of Liam. He wanted to cry out the name. He wanted to cry.

'Well, go on,' he said to himself, 'blub like a baby about it and it'll make everything all right, won't it?' The police would be used to that sort of thing no doubt. His mother would try to comfort him but nobody, not even Nona, could understand the panic of loss he was experiencing now. He sat up straight, his eyes burning again, hard with grief.

They were finally informed that contact had been established with a special squad of rescue police from the city. A swarm of helicopters had been sent in to the Settlement, reinforced by land support. Sent to what? Rod wondered. Had the mad Pastor burnt down the houses of the Settlement? Or something much worse? He had to wait, wait, wait!

The young officer said, in a voice like a pilot consoling a doomed cabin of passengers, that they were in radio contact now and would keep them updated but it would be more sensible if they all went home to get some sleep. They'd be needed in the morning for fuller statements etc etc. But Rhonda dallied, hoping there'd be some early news that would allow them to get the rest they so needed. Nona was silent. They were all hunched up with waiting. Even Vaughan—Rod could make him out through the ugly burls of glass—was hunched over the phone. Had been like that for the last ten minutes. Talking to his oldies who'd run out on him, it seemed. Well, if anything would bring them running back, this should!

'Quite often there's delusion about a perfect place, often another planet,' one of the officers who'd brought them stiff cups of styrafoamed-flavoured coffee was talking to his mother.

'I've read quite a bit now, especially about planned mass suicides of these cult religions,' Rhonda agreed. 'Gets me how often one of these demented leaders manages to convince the followers to such an act of self-destruction. The shared conviction they will go to a better place after they go through an earthly death. Dangerous stuff!'

'Well, deadly, yes,' the officer agreed. 'But at least we have notice on this one. And it may not be too late.'

Rod's heart was hammering away. How can they talk about it as if they were discussing the results of a sporting event? This was more like a bushfire. Hungry, horrendous and on the loose! And then at a signal through the wall of not quite transparent glass, Rhonda rose. 'Looks like there might be some news!'

Rod stood up. He had to. 'Getting some air,' he said to Rhonda and left them behind. Outside there was a line of fat hydrangea bushes, great gleaming plates of blue staring at him. He picked at one of the blooms, and a frail coral cluster came off in his hand. He crushed it for the juice, finding the familiar smell, working the flower to a pulp, his nails digging into the flesh of his hand. 'Let him live!' He was chanting now like the mad pig Pastor. But his was a chant for *life* not for death. 'Let him live.' He whispered the words out loud to the hydrangea blooms that seemed to bob on the breeze, unconcerned.

His mother told him the news, bursting out of the doorway of the small police station, the light behind her making her unruly hair seem like a spurt of yellow flames. 'They have him. Oh my God, they have him, Rod. The Pastor! They have that madman!' and she was laughing and crying. 'They're getting the families out of there right now!'

Nona was there beside her. He waited for her to say the word. Liam. There was silence. He looked from one to the other. Then Nona threw her arms round Rod and he felt her tears on his cheek.

'Some of the boys have holed up in the cellar under the hotel. They have guns. An arsenal of them. Police are trying to reason with them. The place is a time bomb, Rod—guns bullets and petrol. You saw it!'

'No!' Now he was angry. 'What about Liam then?'

'Liam's leading the group. He's saying he wants to fight it out to the end. He won't listen,' and she began sobbing. 'He won't listen to anybody.'

Now it was his turn to comfort. 'It'll be all right,' he soothed, automatically looking over Nona's head into his mother's worried eyes, a splinter of ice in his heart now. 'It'll work out. Liam will see reason. He has to!'

'They got the Pastor up at the church,' Rhonda told him. 'He was trying to collect or get rid of stuff. No one knows. A trunkful of evidence you'd wonder why he'd keep! Photos and diaries and newspaper articles.

'It seems he was on the run. Some religious group he set up in America. He'd embezzled the funds and someone had got wind of it and was after him.' She went on, calmer now. 'He'd got the so-called Inner Circle at the Compound organised in case of attack. Set up the cellar to fight it out when and if 'the enemy' came. One of the boys from the Nooan home wanted out, could see the Pastor was dangerous, what he was up to. He's the one telling the police everything now.

'One of the 'copters came in early, ahead of the rest. It landed right on the hill in the yard of the church. Pastor couldn't make it back down the hill...'

'But Liam,' Rod said urgently.

'Yeah, Liam,' and Nona dropped her head.

'They'll talk him out of it. The squad have experts, specially trained in this sort of thing. Liam will listen.'

'Maybe.' Rod stared out into the darkness.

'Vaughan's still talking to his parents in there. As soon as he's finished we'll go back to the motel,' Rhonda said. 'Better let him know about his grandmother, Rod.'

'Nah, you tell him Nona.'

Rod sat on the grass alone, feeling the wash of cold night air. He felt calmer now they had some news. But a heaviness persisted, the feeling that he'd never see Liam again. They'd try to talk it out but the raggedy little group of boys—Dyson and Tom Vee and the Nooan crew—they would think they were part of an action movie with Liam the hero. It would end in a fight, wouldn't it? Maybe in death. Then a thought occurred to him, an idea that took hold and made him jump to his feet. He paced up and down in front of the hydrangeas, excited, purposeful.

Liam and he had a bond like no other, didn't they? Something he'd never actually been able to voice, something he'd tried to ignore when Liam spoke to him about things...Something Rod had always thought a surf or a dive would wash away as it usually did for him.

They shared the bond of deep guilt. Yes, Rod had felt an enormous guilt about the death of his father, no matter what anyone had said to him about the inevitability of something so dreadful happening in one of his father's increasingly manic phases.

He'd been late home, hadn't he? Dallying with friends, ignoring his absent mother's anxious words, having fun, and then arriving late. Too late! He'd been the one to find his father. He'd been the one who'd shielded Nona from seeing the dreadfulness of that act of violence, because that's what it had been. And he'd been the one who'd tried to bury the guilt and the shame and the extraordinary pain of that death at the bottom of the ocean. In the dark, slimy tunnels, unknowable labyrinths. Down so deep as to never see the light of day. But he'd found it couldn't be submerged far enough. You could never leave the hot searing truth behind you, no matter how fast you swam, how loudly you laughed or how hard you played! Whatever you did it was there, waiting, always ready to surface. He couldn't escape it, the guilt about his father. Just as Liam couldn't escape Benny. *That* was the unspoken bond between them, maybe a precious bond between them. Because, clearly, it was time for Rod to finally voice it. If only he could face up to his own truth, he could perhaps do something for his friend.

He'd go back there to the Settlement, a place he thought he'd never see again. He'd go with the contingent of police he knew were about to take off. He'd ask, no he'd insist, on taking part in whatever thay were planning as part of the rescue operation. Obviously they'd talk to Liam, try to reason with him, persuade him out of the subterranean cellar and back into real life. Well, *he* had things to say to Liam. Amazing things, necessary things, frightening though they were to him. And he knew that what he'd be disclosing to Liam, and to the whole world, might be the thing that would make the difference. He was the *only* one, he concluded, who could find this critical point of connection with Liam—the only one. If he could only brave it. He had to brave it! 'Don't think about it, Chi, just bloody do it!' he said to the pale bobbing flowers. And then he was on his way inside.

∎

In the small room the young sergeant smiled as he handed Vaughan the phone. 'It was pretty easy to track them down after Mrs Chi gave me the name of one of their hotels. They have a manager over here. I got hold of her and, well...'

'Who?' Vaughan asked, frightened it might be something to do with the Pastor.

Rhonda smiled at him. 'We found your parents. At least the police did. When you left so quickly we realised you hadn't been able to raise them. Go on, you can speak to them this time. We'll be back in a few minutes.'

He stared at the phone, so many thoughts racing through his mind. Vaughan felt almost paralysed. The young sergeant placed the receiver firmly in Vaughan's hand and then sat him down on a chair. Vaughan didn't hear him go.

'Vaughan, is that you love? We've just heard the God awful story. We can't believe it's true. Might have been another Jonestown massacre. But you got away. Are you all right? Vaughan?'

'Mum?'

'Are you okay, love? Your father and I got such a shock. Here we are thinking you're having the time of your life.' She paused.

'It *was* just about my life,' he tried to joke but his voice was shaky with emotion.

'That's what the policeman just told me. Imagine January being so easily influenced like that. I just hope they can reach her, get her out of there. He said the fire brigade and police have gone in there. You're father's that upset about her.'

'Yeah, it's terrible!' He wondered if Jasper was upset about him, too.

'Where are you guys now?' he asked, hoping they'd say they'd gone bust and they were in Sydney, somewhere close.

'We're in Las Vegas, love. Your father and I have a few gigs here. Going pretty well. Crazy sort of place, you'd hate it. Neon lights everywhere, gambling casinos, that kind of thing.'

He looked out the window at the dancing signs along the street. 'No, I wouldn't hate it,' he said, 'I reckon I could feel quite at home.'

'We're coming home soon, given what's happened. Real soon.' His heart felt it was about to explode. She was going to make an excuse, talk about her wretched gigs.

'Can I speak to Dad?'

'Love you, Vaughan,' she said anxiously and he didn't know whether to believe it or whether she was being dramatic, saying the right thing, the way she could.

'Yeah,' he said.

He looked up as Nona opened the door a fraction. 'Hey, Vaughan,' she smiled at him. 'Just to let you know they got the Pastor. Your gran's fine.' That was all she said and then she was gone. His father's voice consumed his attention.

'Hullo mate, what a time you've had. Unbelievable what can happen in the space of a few months. That madman and you in the middle of it. What a shocker. We heard the whole ghastly tale. You've got guts, mate. A real Roberts, you are for sure. Vaughan Jasper Roberts the Third, you're a winner!'

It all sounded so hearty and so fake. As if he'd say the same kind of thing to a complete stranger, or on a movie set. Vaughan couldn't speak.

'The police say they'll have everyone out of there in a few hours. They're going to keep us posted about Mum, thank God. They reckon she'll be okay but you know we'll be waiting on tenterhooks.

'It's okay, Dad.'

'What's that?'

'I just heard that Nan's okay. They got her out!'

'Well that's good news, son. Hey Viv, January's all right. Kid's just heard! Told you she's a survivor, my old Ma!' And he heard his father's hearty laughter. He didn't join in, though he felt a surge of relief at the news.

'Hey Vaughan, thank God you have that nice woman looking after you, that's a break.'

A break for whom? Vaughan wondered. Say it. Tell him you can't wait another moment to see them. Tell him they have to come home now!

'Yeah but...' his voice died away.

'You okay?'

He knew all his father wanted to hear was his assent. Be let off the hook as he usually let them off the hook.

Sure, he could say, I'm fine, Dad, and then hear a string of their promises again.

'Vaughan, you there? You okay?'

'No Dad, I'm not bloody okay! I want to see you. I want to see Mum,' he blurted out.

'Hey, of course, soon as we can. We plan to—'

There was that vagueness in his father's voice, despite his surprise, the same tone he'd used when he'd told Vaughan about his 'holiday' at the Settlement this year, with a grandmother he hadn't seen in ten years. 'A few weeks, mate—no more, I promise you.'

'Don't bullshit me, Dad. I don't want to hear any more promises. Six weeks to six months. I want to know what the hell's going on with you two.'

'What do you mean, what's going on?'

'I'm your son, aren't I?' His voice was rising and he didn't care if they could hear him outside. He wouldn't be fobbed off any more.'I need you home now! I deserve to see you now!'

There was a long pause. 'You sound a bit het up, mate.'

'If you mean I know what I want, then yeah, I'm het up. Yeah, you might say that, Dad! Real het up. I feel like you've left me in the lurch, you know that? That you don't really give a damn!'

'Hey Vaughan, we wouldn't do that.'

'So when are you coming home then?'

'See, there's months of work here now for us. Matter of fact we're on tonight and every night this week. But that doesn't mean we won't make arrangements to come back a while. Specially if Mum needs some help and support— though she's pretty tough, that one.'

He didn't speak. He wasn't going to make it easy for his dad. Already he could hear what was about to happen, the big get-out again.

'Maybe you could come to us. Yes, that's what we'll do, in couple of weeks, maybe. Police say you'll be needed—

court case and all. Well, you don't really need us there for that, if January's okay. And this Mrs Chi is willing to—'

Vaughan's heart sank. They'd never change. If they wouldn't come now then they'd never come.

Sure thing, he was about to agree, because he was so tired now and it was useless trying to say anything more to them. Give in. Give up with them. Whatever...Then he heard the receiver snatched from his father's hand.

'Tomorrow, Vaughan.' Her voice, high and excited like it could be when she'd decided something real quick. 'We'll be buying the tickets tomorrow and to hell with this crummy job we have here. We'll head home tomorrow. I promise you that, be with you for the court case and all.' There was such conviction in her voice he had to, he just had to believe her.

'Twenty-four hours then, Mum?' She couldn't see the tears welling in his eyes.

'About that, yes. Give or take a day to get on board, I guess. But we'll phone you first thing, soon as we have reservations. You'll have January there by then I hope. So don't worry about another thing, Vaughan. We're coming home now and that's that!'

He could hear his father blustering in the background. 'Jesus, Viv, I was about to tell the kid that.' It was almost funny except Vaughan felt he wanted to cry.

'We're coming home, Vaughan,' she repeated.

'Good. I...Mum? I've missed you,' and then he couldn't hold back his tears. 'I've missed you real bad.' He took control of his voice somehow. 'Both of you.'

'We've missed you too, darling,' his mother said. 'You've been through horror when you should have been here with us. But you've come through it okay, that's the main thing. Now sleep tight tonight and think of this. We'll be winging our way to you, tomorrow. Okay? Your dad wants to say something.'

'Vaughan,' his father cleared his throat. 'Don't think I haven't thought about you, son. Course I have.'

'Dad, I'm sorry I yelled at you. It's just that—'

'We've gotta go on stage in five minutes—less. But I wanted to say,' and here his father cleared his throat in that awkward way again and Vaughan knew what he was going to say next was not fake at all, 'I want you to know, whatever you think about us being away from you so long, that we both love you.' A long pause. 'That I love you very much.'

'Dad.' His father had never said anything like it before and it was as sweet as that first breath from the airtank, way back there, a hundred years ago. Sweeter.

'And we'll be seeing you soon!' his father's voice was husky and he had to strain to hear. 'Gotta go now. Bye mate.' His mother's voice was still calling out in the background, 'Winging our way!'

Vaughan put his head down on the desk after he'd hung up but it wasn't in defeat. Tomorrow. Winging their way. It sounded so soothing. Beautiful! Winging their way home at last. Winging their way to him. Perhaps it was a lie, like a lot of their other lies. But maybe this time, just maybe, it was the truth. Winging their way home. Tomorrow.

He sat up.

He could laugh now, cry now, just laugh.